the
Perfect
man

the Perfect man

Adapted by Jenny Markas

Based on the motion picture screenplay by Gina Wendkos.

Motion picture story by Michael McQuown &

Heather Robinson & Katherine Torpey.

Scholastic Inc.

New York   Toronto   London   Auckland   Sydney

Mexico City   New Delhi   Hong Kong   Buenos Aires

ISBN 0-439-75378-3

Published by Scholastic Inc.
SCHOLASTIC and associated logos are trademarks and/or registered trademarks of Scholastic Inc.

12 11 10 9 8 7 6 5 4 3 2 1   5 6 7 8 9/0

Designed by Pamela Darcy
Printed in the U.S.A.
First printing, July 2005

Holly Hamilton tapped out a quick blog entry — just a few funny lines about the pop quiz she'd blown in Spanish class — and logged out just as the last bell rang. As she left the computer lab, she spotted her friend Marjorie.

They started pushing their way through the crowded hallway together, Marjorie blending in with the masses in her jeans and T-shirt, and Holly standing out in her one-of-a-kind retro-meets-GAP-meets-punk outfit. Her funky boots alone were enough to guarantee that she'd never be mistaken for a conformist.

"So," Marjorie babbled, "I was all fired up. Finally, a decent spring break! But no, turns out we're not going to *fun* Florida." She bumped up against a skinny kid in glasses, spun back to face Holly, and kept talking. "She's dragging me to my great-aunt's condo in Vero Beach Retirement Nightmare Florida." Marjorie put major spin on her description of the condo, making a horror-movie face.

Holly shrugged. "Vero Beach isn't so bad."

"How do you know?" Marjorie asked as they exited through the main doors and started down the stairs.

"We lived there for a while," Holly told her. "They have manatees. Manatees are cool."

"Wait," Marjorie said, stopping to look at her new friend. "You lived in Florida, too?"

"I told you," Holly said patiently. "I've lived everywhere."

Marjorie slung her backpack over her shoulder and started to walk again. "I don't know how you put up with that. Having to start all over in every new place. Don't you miss your friends?"

Holly shrugged again. "No. This way I get to have friends everywhere."

Marjorie nodded, but Holly could tell she didn't believe what she was hearing.

Just then, the girls started to pass a group of guys hanging out by the bike rack. Holly didn't know any of the guys by name, but she knew their type. They'd been at every school she'd ever attended. Boys like this were the same everywhere. She put her chin up and stepped a little faster, trying to get Marjorie past them before they started in.

"Hey," said one of them, a guy with brown hair flopping into his eyes. "Nice shoes, weirdo!" He pointed at Holly's boots. "Is it Halloween?"

Marjorie gripped her backpack strap and looked away as the other boys laughed. Holly could tell that Marjorie was wishing she could disappear.

But Holly had other ideas. She walked right up to the boy, enjoying the panicked look that crossed his face as she got closer. "Yeah, that's right," she said to him. "I'm a new student here. Thanks for making me feel so comfortable. Usually, kids make fun of new students to make themselves feel better because they're insecure." She waited a beat, watching him squirm. "Thanks for not being a cliché," she finished, speaking into the dead silence. Then she walked away.

Meanwhile, at the A&P supermarket downtown, a woman who looked a lot like a grown-up version of Holly — minus the funky boots, and plus a wild mop of hair — was putting the finishing touches on a truly amazing work of art.

"You should be working at one of them Madame Tussard's places," breathed a fellow bakery employee as she stared at Jean Hamilton's handiwork. "That looks real enough to play with."

It was true. Jean was a master with the cake-decorating tools, and this was one of her best creations ever. It looked *exactly* like a real basketball. But it was going to taste a whole lot better.

"It's for Sean," Jean said, having a hard time keeping the pride out of her voice.

"What's it, his birthday?" asked the other woman.

Jean shook her head. "Our six-month anniversary," she reported. "He called last night and said he had something to talk to me about."

"Ooooh," sighed the woman. "Jean, this could be it!"

"Shh!" Jean said, putting a finger to her lips. "Don't jinx it." She picked up her pastry bag to add one more detail.

As Jean was easing the cake onto a platter, her manager approached. "You got one handsome fella waiting up front," the woman told her.

"*Handsome* and *waiting*," Jean said with a smile. "Two of my favorite words." She checked her smile in the reflection of a big metal spoon. "Wish me luck!" she said as she picked up the cake and headed for the front of the store.

Sean was standing there, looking handsome as ever. And — *nervous*.

Jean came toward her boyfriend, smiling broadly as she held the cake high. But when she was close enough to see his face, her smile faded. "Uh-oh," she said, almost to herself. "I know that look."

At that very moment, Holly and Marjorie were walking down Main Street. "Oh, hey," Marjorie said. "Rosie's dad is loaning her his car to drive to Tulsa for the Pink concert. You got your ticket, right?"

"Not yet," Holly admitted.

"What are you waiting for?" Marjorie asked. "The show is in two weeks."

Holly stopped walking and turned to her friend. "Did you know that there are insects that get born, live a full life, and die in less time than that?"

Marjorie stepped back. She still wasn't totally used to the way Holly thought. "What are you talking about?"

"I'm just saying," Holly said, a little wearily, "a lot can happen in two weeks."

Holly would not have been at all surprised to see what was happening to her mom, back at the A&P.

"What is it?" Jean asked Sean. "You seem nervous."

Sean took a breath. "I cheated on you," he blurted out. "I'm so sorry."

Jean flinched. Then she struggled to recover. "Oh," she said, trying to keep her voice from shaking. "Well, at least you told me. We can get through this. When did it happen?"

"It happened last weekend," Sean told her, ". . . and for three months before that. I'm so glad you understand."

Thirty seconds later, Sean was running down the street outside the A&P with Jean chasing after him, flinging gobs of cake and icing. Sean's face was so covered with frosting, he could hardly see where he was going.

"I understand that you are a two-timing psycho!" shrieked Jean as she threw one last handful of A&P's finest devil's food cake. Then she stood, defeated, watching him go.

Later that afternoon, Marjorie and Holly found their way to Holly's house. Holly pulled out her key and put it in the lock — but stopped before she turned it. There was no mistaking what she heard from inside. Patsy Cline, the queen of the heartbreaker country song, was wailing on the stereo. Holly's shoulders slumped and her face went blank. Then, almost as quickly, she covered up with a smile. She turned to Marjorie. "See?" she asked. "If I'd bought a ticket, I'd be out forty bucks."

"What do you mean?" Marjorie asked, mystified again.

"Patsy's back," Holly explained. "It's packing time."

"Patsy who?" Marjorie asked, bewildered. "Packing where?"

Holly just reached out and gave Marjorie a hug. "Put me on your buddy list," she said. Then she pushed open the door and stepped inside, leaving a confused Marjorie on the doorstep.

The kitchen was almost completely packed up already. All the dishes, all the pots and pans, and most of the glassware were boxed. Jean had the routine down.

As Holly walked in, Jean was dumping a bouquet of wilted flowers out of a china vase. Patsy Cline was deep into her signature song, "Crazy."

"Where are we going this time?" Holly asked.

Jean didn't even look up. She reached for some well-used bubble wrap to cushion the vase. "You're not gonna believe this," she said brightly. "Remember Dolores? Who

I worked with in Chapel Hill? The one who moved back to New York?"

Holly just waited patiently. She knew her mom would get to the point eventually.

"Well," Jean went on, "she told me to keep in touch, so I called her today and she said that the Brooklyn store has an opening."

"So," Holly said. "Brooklyn."

Jean ignored the flat tone of her daughter's voice. "*And*," she went on cheerfully, "her sister just moved in with her boyfriend and wants to sublet her place, so we even have a place to live already!" Triumphantly, she stuck the mummified vase into a box and closed the flaps. Then, and only then, she looked up at Holly.

"Sounds . . . perfect," Holly said. She didn't bother to paste on a smile.

Jean gave her a pleading look. "I'm sorry, baby," she said. "I know you were starting to make friends here."

"No biggie," Holly said lightly. "Kids are everywhere." Avoiding her mother's eyes, she turned and headed into the bedroom she shared with her little sister.

Zoe was packing her stuffed animals. Carefully, she lifted each one off the bed and nestled it into a box. Zoe was only seven, but she already knew how to make a bedroom seem like home. She'd even put up pictures over her bed, something Holly never bothered to do.

Zoe looked at Ivan, her favorite teddy bear, who wore a green sweater. "Is it cold in New York?" she asked.

"Beats me," Holly said as she headed to her desk. The only thing on it was her laptop, and she folded its lid and started to pack it into its case.

Jean came in without knocking. She was carrying an empty suitcase. She knelt on the floor to start packing Zoe's clothes, opening one drawer after another. The room was silent for a few minutes. Then Jean started to talk. "You guys realize how lucky we are?" she asked as she folded a yellow

T-shirt. "Most people don't have the courage to go out and explore new worlds."

Zoe sat back on her heels. "Are we going away because Sean didn't like you, Mommy?" she asked.

Ouch. Jean tried to smile. "Sean liked me," she said. "He just liked other people, too. And we're not going away, baby, we're going *to*. The fact that we're doing so just as I came to my senses about Sean is pure coincidence."

Holly rolled her eyes. "Just like how we left Beaumont, Texas, right when you and Fred, the oh-so-famous poet, called it quits?"

Jean gave Holly a look. "Fred was published," she said.

"*Self*-published, on his laptop," Holly shot back. "Not to mention married."

Zoe had been deep in thought. Now she spoke up. "Was Fred the one that sat on my lizard and killed him?" she asked.

"No, that was Craig," Jean said gently. You could tell she

still felt bad about the lizard incident. "But it was a very old lizard, Zoe, and now where is he?"

"Lizard Heaven?" Zoe asked.

Jean nodded and stuffed the last shirts into the suitcase. "That's right," she said. "I don't know about you, but I'm excited to be getting out of this cow town. Wichita's boring! It's time to shake things up, have a new adventure!" She leaned on the suitcase's lid and snapped it shut. Then she dusted off her hands and left the room.

Zoe had her eyes closed, thinking. "A-D-V-E-N-T-U-R-E," she spelled after a moment. It always made her feel better when she could spell something.

"Yup," said Holly. "Adventure. Mom's word for running away."

username: **GIRL ON THE MOVE**

i'm listening to: **Born to Run**

current mood: **unsettled**

Hey, all you bloggers, sorry for going AWOL. . . .
Holly stared out the window, watching Missouri roll by as
the Hamilton women rattled down the interstate in their
old Jeep, a chunky U-Haul trailer bringing up the rear. She
was composing her next blog entry in her head, figuring
she'd do it for real next time she was anywhere near a DSL
hookup. Not that she'd seen one in the last three days.
Apparently Motel 6 hasn't heard of DSL yet. . . .

Holly reached into the bag for another handful of chips. At least that was one good thing about being on the move: Jean always believed that road trips meant road *food*. Zoe reached up from the backseat to dip in for her own handful.

I saw sixty-three roadkills in Missouri alone. . . . Holly was still composing when suddenly Zoe shrieked in her ear. "T-I-C! Tick!"

"Good one!" said her mom, noting the license plate on the Subaru next to them. It read TIC457. "How about another word with T-I-C?"

Zoe thought for a second. "Stick!" she said triumphantly.

Jean looked over at Holly, who was still staring blankly out the window. "Come on, Little Mary Sunshine," she said to her daughter. "Give us a word with T-I-C in it."

"Tragic," offered Holly without missing a beat. She turned her blank look on her mother.

Jean managed a smile. "Fantastic," she offered in return.

Holly couldn't help herself. A tiny smile tugged at the corner of her lips. "Pathe*tic*," she answered back.

This time, Jean frowned. As much as she liked word games, this one wasn't making her happy.

Holly tried again. "Ecsta*tic*," she said.

"Thank you," said Jean with a grin.

"Sarcas*tic*," Holly added.

Jean raised her eyebrows. She wasn't about to give up without a fight. "Psycho*tic*," she countered.

"It's gene*tic*." Holly couldn't let her have the last word.

Jean was silent for a second. "Ooh, I've got one," she said suddenly. "*Tic*kle!" With that, she snaked out her right hand and started tickling Holly's belly.

"Hey!" Holly said, giggling. She was *the* most ticklish person on the planet, and her mother knew it. "Don't do that while you're driving! It's not safe!"

But Jean couldn't be stopped. "Erra*tic*! Spas*tic*! Ero*tic*!

Despotic! I am the queen of this game!" Keeping her eyes on the road, she kept tickling until Holly was breathless with laughter.

Later — *much* later, somewhere about three states away — Holly mentally composed another entry for her blog as she watched her mother flirt with the tall, serious state trooper who had just pulled them over. **By some miracle, my mom only got one speeding ticket the whole drive. I wish irrational thinking was illegal, because then she would be so busted. . . .**

It was early morning when they trundled across the Brooklyn Bridge. Holly was driving by that time, while both her mom and sister slept soundly. **I will say one thing, though,** she thought, knowing she wanted to share the amazing sight she was seeing. **For those of you who haven't done it yet, put "Must See New York Skyline" on your list of Things To Do Before I Die.**

Holly drank in the sight of the morning sun glinting off skyscrapers and touching the river with gold. Maybe New York wouldn't be so bad after all.

"Hey, wake up," Holly said to Jean and Zoe as she pulled the Jeep up in front of a crumbly old brownstone on a wide street shaded with trees. It couldn't have looked any more different from their place in Wichita, but Holly had to admit that something about it looked almost — well, *homey*.

Jean was even more enthusiastic. "Ooh, girls," she said as she climbed out of the car and looked up at the building. "I bet it's full of quaint details like pretty moldings on the ceiling and old hardwood floors."

They climbed the outside stairs and stood at the top of the stoop. Jean rang the bell, and a short, dumpy woman — the landlady — greeted them and led them up the stairs. "This is it," she said, opening the door of an apartment and ushering them in.

There wasn't a quaint detail in sight.

The apartment was cramped and tiny, like every place they'd ever had. Holly took in the dingy kitchenette. "And charming little rat droppings in the breakfast nook!" she said gaily. "It's delightful."

"Cut it out," Jean told her briskly. "It's charming! A perfect blank slate to make our own!" With that, she dumped the box she was carrying onto a dusty counter.

The three Hamilton women spent the rest of the day unpacking. Zoe lined up her stuffed animals carefully, arranging them exactly the same way she'd arranged them in Wichita, in Vero Beach, in Springfield, and in Boulder.

Jean and Holly worked efficiently through the boxes, following a routine they'd established years ago. Jean did the kitchen, while Holly did the bathroom and living room. Soon, everything was in its place in the new space. **The sad thing is,** Holly thought, pre-writing her blog again, **I'm actually getting good at this. If all else fails, I have a very promising future with Bekin Movers.**

They broke for pizza at seven, and by nine they were just about done. As the finishing touch, Jean pulled her pretty vase out of the last box, unwrapped the bubble wrap, and set the vase on the dining room table. From the bottom of the box, she pulled out a small bouquet of silk daisies and plunked it into the vase.

There. They were home.

Holly headed for her room and her laptop, now that she finally had a phone jack to plug into. Jean and Zoe stepped out onto the balcony for one last look at their new city before bed.

"See?" Jean asked, putting her arm around Zoe. She pointed up at the moon, rising full and fat over the jumble of buildings that stretched as far as their eyes could see. "There it is. Same moon as in Wichita," Jean told her daughter. "Still coming out, every night, even in hard times, to remind us that every day holds the potential for beauty."

* * *

Inside, Holly was busy typing.

username: GIRL ON THE MOVE

i'm listening to: unidentified teen female angst music

current mood: overwhelmed

Quickly, she wrote up all the entries she'd composed in her mind. Then, just before she logged off, she added some final words

Anyway. Keep reading. I'll be here. The same me . . . just a different zip code.

Early the next morning, Holly, Jean, and Zoe found themselves outside on the street, studying a map of their adoptive
borough. It didn't take long for Holly to figure out where she
was heading next. She kissed her mother, gave her little sister
a pat on the head, and took off without looking back.

Her new school looked imposing. It wasn't so much the
building, though it *was* quite the pile of rock. It was more the
student body. When Holly walked up to the entrance, she
had to weave her way through clumps of tough-looking
kids. The Puerto Ricans were on one side, laughing and kidding one another about their outfits. On the other side

were the African-American kids, a bunch of whom were playing dice against a wall.

Holly gazed around, trying to figure out where she was going to fit in, if anywhere. Suddenly, and totally by mistake, she stepped on one of the dice.

"Yo, yo, yo!" yelled one of the kids.

"Oops, sorry!" Holly blushed and quickstepped away from the group.

"Hey, you!" called a voice. "Yeah, *you*!"

Holly turned around. Was someone calling *her*?

"What'd your hoofs cost you?" asked a girl with brown hair and a classic Brooklyn accent.

"What?" Holly had no idea what she was talking about.

Then the girl pointed down at her own feet. She was wearing the exact same boots as Holly's, and they went well with her retro outfit of a cardigan and skirt. "I paid fifty bucks for mine," the girl said. "You?"

Holly grinned. "Free. Pulled 'em out of a garbage can somewhere in Portland."

"You win," said the girl. She trotted over to catch up with Holly. "I'm Amy Pearl. You're new, huh?"

"Holly Hamilton," Holly said. "How'd you know I was new?"

"Your skin," Amy said.

Holly blinked. "My skin looks new?" she asked, bewildered.

"It looks virgin," Amy explained. "No tats, no piercings. Brooklyn girls lose their skin virginity by fifth grade."

Holly laughed. She liked this girl. "And to think in fifth grade I was only learning long division."

Amy laughed, too. The girls joined a long line of students that snaked out from the main entrance. "Okay," said Amy, "first piece of advice. If you're hiding any knives or guns, they usually find 'em."

"If I'm *what*?" Holly asked. Then she saw what Amy was talking about. Up ahead, there was a series of complicated-looking gates: metal detectors, just like the ones in airports.

A huge security guard stood nearby. He waved the two girls forward when it was their turn.

Without waiting to be asked, Amy raised both arms so that the guard could sweep a security wand around her body. Holly was so stunned that she just stood there staring, until the guard gently raised her arms for her, taking her bag to lay it on the inspection table. He began to move the wand around.

"So," Amy asked while she waited. "Divorce, death, or bankruptcy?"

"What?" Holly asked. She was beginning to feel as if she were in a foreign country. Normally quick on the uptake, she was baffled by nearly everything she was hearing and seeing. She'd lived in a lot of places, but Brooklyn was definitely something new.

Just then, the guard's wand began to beep. It was hovering near Holly's waist. She stood there, feeling her heart beating fast. What was she supposed to do *now?*

Amy stepped forward and pulled Holly's keys out of her pocket. She tossed them onto the table. "Why you moved," she explained. "Usually, when a kid shows up midsemester, those are the top three reasons: divorce, death, or bankruptcy. So which is it?"

"Oh," Holly said. "All three, if you count my mother's last boyfriend. He was so boring, he might as well have been dead."

Now the wand was beeping again, at Holly's other pocket.

Holly froze.

The guard rolled his eyes.

The kids waiting in line groaned.

Amy reached into Holly's pocket and pulled out a cell phone.

Finally, they were clear. They grabbed their stuff and walked on down the hall. Holly gazed around, trying to take everything in and get her bearings. The girls passed a big poster that read: SENIORS ORDER YEARBOOKS NOW.

"Bummer," Amy said, pointing at the sign. "You're going to have to take your yearbook photo with all the jerks and losers who missed it in the fall."

Holly wasn't looking at the sign. She was puzzling over her class schedule, trying to figure out where she was supposed to be for first period. "I don't do yearbook photos," she said.

"You don't have a choice," Amy informed her. "They're like death and taxes here. Mandatory pain. If you don't do it yourself, they'll hunt you down like an animal and force you to smile."

"Not if I'm not here anymore, they won't," Holly said, still frowning at her schedule. "Which way is Room C-103?"

Meanwhile, across Brooklyn in an A&P bakery department that looked a lot like the one in Wichita, Jean was getting the grand tour. Her friend Dolores, who had gotten her the job, explained where things were stashed. ". . . And this is where all the mixers are kept, but I warn you, they're all older than God. They don't really mix anymore, they just kind of . . . move things around." She made a muscle with her right arm and pointed to it, smiling. "So I hope your manual mixer is in good shape! And watch out for this no-good oven," she went on. "It's worse than the one in Chapel Hill. Off by a good ten degrees."

Jean shrugged. "Well, you know me. I'm off by way more than that."

Dolores laughed as she led Jean over to meet another woman, younger than both of them, who was bent over a cake, trying to apply white chocolate petals to its frosting. "And this is Gloria," said Dolores. "Gloria — Jean, the one I was telling you about."

"Real nice to meet you, Gloria," said Jean, with a big smile.

"Likewise," Gloria said. "Welcome to Brooklyn." She picked up a petal and stifled a frustrated sigh. "Why won't this work?" she muttered.

"Hate to be a know-it-all," Jean offered, "but if white chocolate gets too warm, it won't curl."

Gloria's eyes widened.

"See?" Dolores asked. "Told you she was good."

Gloria looked down at her wilted flower and shook her head. "No wonder my white cakes always look so bad. Thank you!"

Back at school, Holly was meeting people, too. Specifically, a boy named Adam Forrest. She saw his name on his notebook as he was trying to kick her out of her seat. She couldn't help noticing that his notebook was also covered with Emily Is Strange stickers. Or that he was dressed like no other boy at this school, in a thrift-store T-shirt, well-worn vintage cords, and a scarf around his neck.

He stared down at Holly, who had carefully chosen a seat in the back of the room for her first English class. "That's my seat," he said.

"There's assigned seating?" Holly asked, surprised. There hadn't been in any of her other classes that morning.

"No. But." Adam just stood there.

Holly craned her neck around him and spotted a few open desks near the front. "Why don't you take one of them?" she asked, pointing.

"I don't like sitting up front," answered Adam.

"Neither do I." Holly just sat there, staring back up at him.

Finally, Adam seemed to realize that she wasn't going to move. He rolled his eyes and plopped down at a desk in the next row forward, right in front of Holly. When he pulled out a sketch pad, she had a good view of some pretty good anime comics. She stared, impressed, as he started to sketch another panel.

Adam turned around and caught her looking.

Holly looked away.

Adam turned back and started to draw again.

Holly watched until the teacher, a round-faced man

wearing a classic absentminded-professor tweed jacket accessorized with a bow tie, came in and closed the door behind him. According to Holly's class schedule, this was Mr. Orbach.

"Good day, students," he said. "Today's debate topic is 'Broadcast Decency Laws. Do they protect children?' Dexter, I'd like you to take the pro position. Come on up."

A boy in Holly's row stood up, hitched up his low-riding pants, adjusted his baseball cap, and slouched to the front of the class. "Word up," he said, grinning, "I'm a pro. Steady-ballin' playa!"

Every student in the class cracked up.

Dexter nodded, acknowledging his fans. "Yo, yo, yo, check it," he went on. "The pro that flows from mullets —" He pointed to a kid in front with a major blond mullet. "To afros —" He pointed at a 'fro wearer near the radiator. Then he went into his rap:

"Moms buys your clothes and food 'til you grows

Don't test her will, 'cause, homey, she knows

The violence and cussin' ain't right for kids, yo

You got Dex catch wreck from droppin' dope prose!"

"Yeah!" the class broke into yells and applause.

"All right," said a frowning Mr. Orbach. "Settle down." He turned to Dexter. "Next time, Dexter, let's lose the rhyme and the lingo so everyone can understand what you're talking about. I shouldn't need an interpreter. Who would like to argue against Dexter's position?"

Nobody spoke up.

Mr. Orbach glanced around the room. Not one student made eye contact. Then he spotted Holly. "How about our new addition to the class?" He checked his ledger. "Holly Hamilton? Would you please come up and present an opposing argument?"

Holly was trapped, and she knew it. Slowly, she stood up,

feeling every eye in the class on her. Ick. There's nothing like being the new kid. She glanced across the room to where Amy was sitting. At least there was one familiar face in the room. "Uh," she began.

Mr. Orbach jumped right in. "'Uh' is not a good opening to any argument, Holly."

Holly looked at him. Fine, if he was going to be mean about it, she wouldn't hold back. "Actually," she said, "there's no need for me to make an argument. You proved my point for me."

Stunned silence filled the room.

Mr. Orbach glared at Holly, speechless.

Before he could say anything, she went on. "Dexter laid out a solid case using language everyone in this room understands and relates to. Everyone except you."

Nobody moved a muscle. They all looked at Mr. Orbach, waiting to see what he would say now.

He cleared his throat. "Go on."

Holly nodded. "People your age don't even understand how kids our age talk, much less what we're about. So how can you make a judgment on something you don't get? And, more to the point, have no interest in getting?"

Dexter was nodding righteously. Some of the kids were starting to chuckle.

Mr. Orbach raised an eyebrow. "Please continue."

Holly didn't hesitate. "You adults all complain that our generation isn't being raised with good values. Well, who's to blame? DJs? Cable TV? I don't think so."

Adam put down his pencil and looked at Holly. He was smiling. A ripple of laughter began to run through the room as everyone caught on to Holly's point.

"I think it's you," Holly went on. "You raised us. You're the ones with the fifty-percent divorce rate. You're the ones who keep making the same mistakes over and over again.

But I guess it's easier to blame it on naked butts on TV and dirty DJs than it is to look at yourself and say, 'Maybe *I'm* the problem. Maybe I can't raise my child because I *am* a child. It's time for me to grow up.'" Holly took a deep breath. "Maybe then you'll understand that the TV isn't the bad parent. It's you."

She stopped and sat down. The classroom was so quiet, you could hear the clock's second hand clicking.

"Well done," said Mr. Orbach finally. "Welcome to class."

By late afternoon, Jean was well into the swing of things at the bakery. She and Gloria were stocking the cookie bins when Jean caught a glimpse of Gloria's flashy engagement ring. "It's gorgeous!" she said.

"It's so heavy, I need a crane to lift my finger," Gloria bragged.

"Baby," Dolores said, walking by with a tray of cream

puffs, "if he is any good, you'll never need to lift a finger again."

"I'm so glad I listened to you." Gloria smiled at Dolores. "He was a customer," she explained to Jean. "Dolores coached me through the whole thing. When to give him an extra doughnut, when to hold back . . ."

Dolores nodded. "It's just like with fish: Reel him in, then give him some play, reel in, give him play. . . . Eventually the man's so confused, he buys a rock" — she gestured at Gloria's ring — "just to know what to expect."

Jean put her hands on her hips. "You never told *me* that!"

"Oh, I told you," Dolores said. "You just didn't want to listen." She turned to Gloria. "Jean's the kind that pulls and pulls till the line breaks and the fish swims away as fast as he can." Her back was to Jean now. "What she's gotta do is —"

Just then, Holly spoke up from the other side of the counter, where she'd been standing quietly, listening. "What she's gotta do is sign my enrollment card," she said.

Jean lit up. She checked her watch. "Hey, is it four o' clock already?" she asked. "Girls, this is my daughter Holly."

"Look at you," said Dolores, "all grown up."

"Welcome to Brooklyn, Holly," said Gloria.

"Thanks," said Holly. She looked at her mom. "Can we go?"

"Sure, baby," Jean said, taking off her name tag. "See you tomorrow, girls." She slung an arm around Holly's shoulder as they headed out of the bakery. "How was it?" she asked. "Tell me everything."

Before Holly could say a word, they were interrupted by a smarmy-looking guy wearing a name tag that read LENNY. He blocked the aisle, smiling appreciatively as he looked

Jean up and down. Then he put on a sad face. "Did it hurt?" he asked.

"Did what hurt?" Jean replied, impatient to hear about Holly's day.

"When you fell from heaven?" Lenny delivered his line with a smug smile. "'Cause with a face like that, you gotta be an angel."

Holly rolled her eyes, but Jean cracked up. "Has that line ever worked for you?"

Lenny smirked. "Got you to laugh, didn't I? That's step one."

Jean saw her opening. "So, you were making a joke when you said I had the face of an angel?"

"No —" said Lenny. She had him all confused. "I was just . . . saying . . ." He gave up. "Oh, you're good. You're gonna make me work hard, aren't you?" He stuck out a hand and introduced himself. "Lenny Horton. Bread Manager."

"I'm Jean. This is my daughter Holly." Jean gave Holly a little push forward.

"How you doin', Holly?" Lenny smiled at her.

"Great," Holly said flatly. "Come on, Mom. We're due back in heaven."

First days at new schools all feel the same. Like you're suddenly on a new planet, breathing a new atmosphere . . .

Holly was in the middle of a sentence later that night when Jean tapped on her door and came in. She was carrying a picture of herself. "Can you scan this into the computer so I can put it online?" Jean asked.

"Mom," Holly said, "I'm *busy*!"

"Doing what?" asked Jean, trying to catch a look at the screen.

Holly closed the lid of her laptop. "Do you have to do

this right now? Why don't you just wait this time and see if you meet someone the normal way?"

Jean took hold of Holly's arm and pulled her out of her chair. She drew her over to a mirror on the wall and pointed to her own face. "Have you seen these lines?" she asked. "I'm in a race against time. Get on out there and scan this thing. Every second counts!"

The true bonding moment for Holly and her new friend came the next day during a coed basketball game in gym class, of all things.

Amy and Holly were, not surprisingly, sitting on the bench. They weren't exactly jocks, and it was easy to avoid getting picked for a team. They watched the rest of the class dribble up and down.

"Whatever you do," Amy said, staring at one side of the court, "don't look over there."

"Where?" Holly asked, turning to look.

Amy yanked Holly's head back.

"Ow!" Holly rubbed her head.

"You looked," said Amy.

"I didn't even know at what!" Holly said.

Amy lowered her voice to a whisper. "At Enzo Walker. The biggest jerk in the whole world, with whom I am totally obsessed."

This sounded all too familiar to Holly. "Oh, my god, Amy," she said. "You're my mother." Shaking her head sadly, she looked out at the court.

Then she saw Adam Forrest.

Everybody else on the court was wearing white gym socks and regulation athletic shoes.

Adam? He was wearing argyle socks and Vans. Proudly.

Suddenly, he was looking right back at Holly. Oops. Busted. She ducked her head, but not before she saw him nod at her. She looked up again to see him snag the ball and head for the basket, fooling around with some Harlem Globetrotter—like moves, dribbling around his back and all. He paused to take a shot, and then tossed it up casually, as if to say, "Sure, I'm good, but I don't care." The ball swished through the hoop — nothing but net.

Then he looked back at Holly.

Amy saw the whole thing happen. "Whoa," she said. "Hang it up. Is it my imagination, or is Adam Forrest totally checking you out?"

"It's your imagination," Holly assured her.

"No," said Amy decisively, "I don't have an imaginative bone in my body. He totally is."

"Not interested." Holly looked straight ahead.

"Why not?" Amy asked. "He's fine."

Holly felt herself blush a little. He *was* fine. But then she got a grip. "Romance is overrated," she told her friend. "I mean, sure, it's good terrain for poets or pop songwriters, but for real people? When has it ever worked? Name one couple." She looked at her friend, waiting.

And waiting.

And waiting.

43

Amy took her time trying to think of a successful couple. Finally, she had to give in. She shook her head. "But I still want Enzo Walker," she said.

Holly invited Amy over after school. When they walked in, they found Jean in the living room, eating peanut butter out of the jar and talking back to a TV psychologist while Zoe lay on the floor, doing what passes for homework in second grade.

On the TV, the psychologist was giving a thin, sad woman a really hard time. "How can you be so stupid as to think that man cares about you?" he shouted as the woman sniffled back tears.

"Yeah, but — I just want to know" — she hiccupped — "why he'd walk all over me like that?"

The psychologist ignored her crying. "You can't be walked on if you don't lie down," he preached.

Jean couldn't take any more. "Oh, back off, you bald

idiot!" she yelled at the screen. "The poor woman is sui-
cidal!" Her voice sounded thick and gummy, due to her
mouthful of peanut butter.

"S-U-I-C-I-D-A-L," spelled Zoe helpfully.

Holly cringed but decided to make the best of it. "Mom,
this is Amy," she said.

Jean didn't even look up. She was still staring hatefully at
the psychologist.

"She came over to study," Holly went on.

Jean just nodded.

"She's gonna stay for dinner," Holly added.

Another nod.

"And then we're gonna rob a couple banks."

Again — the nod.

Holly shrugged and led the way to her room.

When she'd closed the door behind them, Amy spoke
up. "Is your mom always like that?" she asked.

"No," Holly said. "Just when she's got DBM."

Amy nodded, as if she knew what that was. Then she had to ask. "Is that like PMS?"

"Deep Bummer Mode," Holly explained. "It's my way of making depression sound catchy." She sat down on her bed and picked up the latest issue of *Rolling Stone*.

"What's she depressed about?" Amy wasn't ready to let the subject drop.

Holly sighed. "She put an ad online last week."

Amy joined her on the bed. "Did anyone answer?"

"She got, like, a hundred responses," Holly reported. She walked over to the computer and punched a few keys. Then she gestured for Amy to come look. "This guy is in prison," she said, pointing to the screen. "So is this guy . . . and this guy . . . and this woman . . . and this guy."

Amy peered at the last picture. "He looks cool," she said.

"He killed his wife," Holly told her. She pulled up another page of photos. "This guy is too heavy to leave the house." *Click.* "This guy wants to buy a wife." She clicked through them quickly. "This guy is from Utah. He wants a wife who can get along with his other wives."

Amy wasn't sure what to say. "At least she got responses."

Suddenly exhausted, Holly closed her laptop, flopped back down on the bed, and said what she'd been thinking for a long, long time. "I think the only way my mom is gonna meet a good man is if she doesn't pick him."

5

COME ONE! COME ALL! PARENT AND STUDENT NIGHT!

The posters were done in fun colors and had lots of exclamation points, as if to convince the reader that the event would be lots and lots of fun.

Holly knew better.

But she had let Jean talk her into attending "as a family." That meant that all three of them got to slip in together, hoping nobody noticed that they were ten minutes late due to a cake crisis at the bakery.

Principal Campbell was already on stage in the gym, going over some of the basic rules she fought an uphill battle to enforce. ". . . And if a student brings a cell phone to school," she was saying, "it will be confiscated regardless of how 'cool' their ring tones are."

Holly noticed Amy and her parents across the gym. Several rows down from her, Adam sat with his mother. Holly gave Amy a tiny wave as she and Zoe followed Jean to some empty seats halfway up the bleachers. "Why are we here?" she asked as she climbed past parents and kids who were already seated. "It's not as if these will be my teachers four months from now."

"Holly," said Jean patiently, "that's negative imaging." She squeezed herself past a large man to a spot where there was room for the three of them, and Holly sat down between her mom and Zoe.

Principal Campbell was introducing an aging-hippie type Holly hadn't seen before. "Now I would like to introduce to you the head of our Guidance Department, Dr. Charles Fitch."

Dr. Fitch didn't look like much. He was skinny, with

longish hair and weird orthopedic-looking shoes. He loped up to the mic. But Holly felt Jean perking up. *A man!* her radar was saying.

"Hey there, everyone," said Dr. Fitch. "Great to see you all. Let me tell you how I run the Guidance Department. I have an open-door policy, which means you can stop by my office whenever you want." He looked around the gym, trying to make meaningful eye contact with as many students as possible. "I also have an open-mind policy: There are no stupid questions. So please, if there's something on your mind, knock on my door . . ."

At that, Jean's hand shot up.

Dr. Fitch couldn't help noticing. You could tell he was a little surprised. He hadn't planned on taking questions right *then*, but why not? ". . . or raise your hand," he finished. "Woman in the back — yes?"

Jean spoke out in a clear, strong voice. "Instead of meetings like this once a year, have you considered a monthly forum where students and teachers can exchange thoughts, in an effort to enhance communication and bridge gaps?"

Holly was surprised. And — proud.

There was a smattering of applause. Holly noticed Adam's mother clapping.

"That's an excellent comment, Mrs. . . ." Dr. Fitch beamed at Jean.

"*Miss*," corrected Jean. "Hamilton."

Suddenly, Holly had a sinking feeling. She knew where this was going.

"I also wondered," Jean said, now that she had the floor, "if you'd thought of a monthly mixer for single parents?"

This time, nobody applauded. Instead, there were a lot of baffled faces as everyone stared at Jean — and at Holly.

Dr. Fitch cleared his throat uncomfortably. "Um," he said.

But Jean barely noticed the reception she was getting.

She was on a roll. "Not that I wouldn't like to meet the married parents, as well. I would. But in some instances," she rattled on, "we single parents have different concerns than the married ones. Different *priorities*, if you know what I mean. And by priorities, I mean, I need to meet a man."

Holly sank lower on the bench, wishing she could drop down through the bleachers.

"So, maybe," Jean went on, oblivious, "we could throw a mixer once a month until some of the single parents become married parents. Or at least until *I* become a married parent." She gave a little laugh.

Other people laughed, too, but it was an uncomfortable, nervous kind of laughter. Holly saw, across the gym, that Adam was laughing.

She wanted to die.

And yet, Jean was still not done. "I'm just kidding," she

said, "but in all seriousness, I just want to say, I'm *not* kidding. I'm deadly serious."

Suddenly, everybody in the place was laughing, really laughing.

Everybody except Holly.

She was still furious later that night. Holly glared into the mirror as she brushed her teeth. Jean came in and leaned against the doorway. She watched as Holly scrubbed away, much harder than is considered necessary for the removal of tartar and plaque.

"You just gonna not talk to me for the rest of your life?" Jean asked.

Brush, brush, brush.

"Oh, come on, Holly," Jean said. "Every unmarried parent there appreciated the suggestion."

At that, Holly whirled around, her mouth full of foam.

She was livid. "Did it ever occur to you that *maybe* the meeting wasn't about the needs of the single parents? That the point of the meeting might have been — oh, I don't know — the *kids?*"

Whoa. Jean considered this. "Well, sure," she said finally. "I was just thinking —"

"About *you*," Holly raged. "All you ever think about is *you.*" She spit out her toothpaste and stomped out of the room.

Holly had cooled down a bit by the time she woke up the next morning, but now her fury was replaced by humiliation. She was tempted to hide under the covers and never again show her face at school. But she had no choice. Jean was never one to allow "mental health" days. She insisted on both her girls going to school every single day, unless they were physically unable to move.

Holly managed to slip into the building without being seen. But as she was rummaging in her locker, Adam came strolling down the hall, straight toward her. Knowing it was impossible to hide, Holly tried anyway, slipping behind her open locker door and closing her eyes.

"You know what the entire student body is talking about this morning?" Adam asked casually.

Oh, she knew all right. Holly winced as she opened her eyes to look at him. She just knew he'd be laughing at her.

But he wasn't. He had a sweet smile on his face instead. "They're talking about the Krispy Kreme truck that got in a wreck on Eighth Avenue," he told her. "Doughnuts every-where. Total free-for-all. Between the excitement and the sugar buzz, everyone's pretty much forgotten about any-thing that happened before eight o'clock this morning." Still smiling, he hitched up his backpack, nodded at her, and headed off for his first class.

Wow. Holly watched him go. Could he really be as nice as he seemed?

Whether it was because of the doughnut truck or not, Holly didn't notice any stares or snickers all day. Maybe everybody at this school was *used* to outbursts like that at parent-teacher meetings.

"No, it's just that we *all* have crazy mothers," Amy told her as they left school later that day. They were walking down the street together. Amy had invited Holly to go get a bite to eat after school. "My mother owns four hundred and thirty-three handbags."

"Yeah," Holly said, "but she didn't bring them all to the school meeting, did she?" She was still a little ticked off at Jean. As they waited for a WALK signal, she went on, "It's always the same. First she's hopeful, and then when the perfect man doesn't appear in two weeks, she gets desperate and hooks up with some loser. Some guy who isn't good enough to mop her floors." She kept babbling as she and Amy went around a corner. "And when it doesn't work out — because it *never* works out — we pack up and move. Again. And there's nothing I can do about it." Her voice was rising. "I can't even run away. She owns that!"

Amy was taken aback. "I thought you said you didn't mind all the moving around," she said.

"I didn't," said Holly. "I mean, I don't. I mean —" Ugh. She knew what she meant. She absolutely, positively, most definitely was sick to death of moving. The idea of packing up those boxes one more time made her — ugh. She sighed deeply. "I just got here," she said finally. She was so deep in her thoughts that it took her a moment to realize that Amy had stopped in front of a restaurant. She looked up at the sign. "The River Bistro?" she asked.

Amy led her inside, and Holly looked around, awed. The place was majorly upscale, the kind of joint where models ate with their billionaire boyfriends. Not that there were any of either in sight at the moment; the restaurant was nearly empty as waiters in white aprons prepared for the dinner rush. "What are we doing here?" Holly hissed to Amy. "I can't afford to *pee* in a place like this, much less order actual food."

Amy laughed. "Relax. It's under control. My uncle Ben's

the owner." She pointed to the open kitchen across the room, where a cute, dark-haired older guy — maybe around Jean's age — was multitasking: talking on the phone while he arranged pots and pans on wire racks.

"How long did you keep her waiting?" he demanded into the phone, as Holly and Amy approached. Spotting Amy, he came over to give her a kiss on the cheek, still chatting. "An *hour*?" he asked. "She's right. You *are* a dog."

"This is Holly," Amy whispered to her uncle.

Ben nodded and led them over to a low freezer, where he began to scoop ice cream into dishes for them. "The only thing you *can* do," he said into the phone as he worked, "flowers." He put a bowl of chocolate ice cream in front of Amy, then turned to Holly. Still listening to the person on the other end, he raised his eyebrows at Holly. "Pistachio, right?" he whispered.

Holly nodded without thinking. Pistachio was her all-time

favorite — in fact, she'd rather have *no* ice cream if pistachio weren't available. But how in the world could this man have guessed? "How did he know that?" she asked Amy, when Ben started to scoop her ice cream.

"He knows females," said Amy, closing her eyes in delight as she ate her first spoonful of chocolate.

Ben put down a heaping dish and a spoon in front of Holly, still talking. "And don't go cheap," he advised his friend. "Top of the line, a full dozen, long stemmed."

Holly took a bite of pistachio and smiled. By now she was listening closely to Ben's conversation.

"Of course it'll work," he was saying. "Roses always work."

Holly rolled her eyes. How simplistic. "He doesn't believe that, does he?" she asked Amy.

Amy just shrugged and took another bite of ice cream.

But Ben had heard the question. He gave Holly a little smile as he finished up with his friend. "Anytime, pal," he said. "Bye." He clicked a key on his phone and slipped it into his pocket. Then he leaned toward Holly. "And yes, I believe that, little lady," he said to her. "You don't?"

"That roses always work?" Holly asked. "No. If the guy's a loser, roses aren't going to change anything. They're just flowers." She didn't see any reason to beat around the rosebush.

Ben gave her a closer look. "Aren't you a little young to be so cynical?"

Amy jumped in. "She doesn't believe in romance," she informed her uncle.

Ben looked back at Holly, nodding. "Then this is for you," he said, pulling a gorgeous, perfect yellow rose out of an arrangement on the bar. He handed it to Holly.

She stared down at the flower in her hand, then looked back at Ben.

"See," he said, "when a woman's been let down by a guy,

it's not just her faith in *him* that's been eroded. It's her faith in the whole concept of love. She's back to thinking she'll have to settle for less than perfect."

He reached out and took the rose back, sniffed it, and closed his eyes for a moment. When he opened them, he went on, "A flower like this, though, it *is* perfect. And giving a woman a dozen of them — it's like saying to her, don't give up. Perfect is out there, waiting for you. You'll find it."

Wow. Holly had to admit that the guy made a good argument. He was more than cute — he was smart and very persuasive. But she wasn't ready to let *him* know that. "A yellow rose says all that, huh?" she asked skeptically.

"Oh, no," said Ben. "No, yellow is for your sick grandmother in the hospital." He thought for a second. "For a woman — red. Or if you really want to knock her socks off, you send her an orchid."

Now Amy was intrigued. She put down her spoon. "Why? What do orchids say?"

Ben smiled and looked off into the distance. "Orchids . . ." he began, "orchids make a woman feel like she's floating on a cloud of infinite possibility. As long as she feels like that, what's there to be depressed about?" He handed the rose back to Holly.

Holly lifted it to her nose and took a deep breath, thinking hard as its sweet fragrance enveloped her.

"I swear, I'll pay you back," Holly said a half hour later. She and Amy were standing in front of a flower stand on a corner near Ben's restaurant. Blooms of every color spilled out of tin buckets, their perfume scenting the air. Holly was counting her money, but no matter how many times she added it up, she didn't have enough for the fabulous fuchsia orchids in the third row of buckets.

"I still don't get how flowers from you will fix things," Amy said, but she dug into her pocket and pulled out a five. She handed it to Holly.

"They're not flowers," Holly explained, "they're *orchids*.

And they're not from me. They're from her perfect man."
She sounded totally sure of herself.

"Then let *him* pay," Amy said, still not getting it.

"I would," said Holly, "if he existed."

"I'm lost," Amy admitted, thinking that the flower perfume must be getting to her friend's brain.

"You heard your uncle," Holly said. "Orchids will tell my mom she's special. Which will make her happy. Which will make me happy. Everybody wins."

She reached into the mass of orchids and pulled out one perfect stem. Then she marched into the shop to pay.

When they got back to her house, Holly paused on the stoop, holding the orchid. "Give me a couple of minutes to get in," she instructed her friend. "Then ring the doorbell and run." Tucking a card into the orchid, she set it underneath the buzzer.

Immediately, Amy saw what she thought was a flaw in

the plan. "Won't your mom just ring the intercom?" she asked.

Holly shook her head. "It's broken. Normally she sends me down to see who's there, but I'll cover somehow and make her go."

Amy nodded, but Holly could tell she was hesitating. "What?" she asked.

"It's just —" Amy paused. "Are you sure this is a good idea?"

Holly waved a hand. "Sure," she said lightly. "A few flowers never hurt anybody." With that, she opened the door and raced upstairs.

This time, there was no TV on. Jean was slumped on the couch, still wearing her A&P uniform. She was doing a crossword puzzle, her favorite stress-relief activity. Nearby, on the floor, Zoe was coloring as she listened to her Walkman.

"Hi, Mom," Holly said, trying to sound casual and not too out of breath.

Jean smiled at her, but her mind was clearly elsewhere. "Marsupial," she muttered, looking down at her clues. "Six letters." She tapped her pen on her teeth. "Possum!" she said, writing it down.

Holly walked into the kitchen. "Boy," she said, wishing she didn't sound as if she were following a script. "Am I thirsty!" She ran herself a glass of water.

Just then, the buzzer rang.

Jean didn't budge.

"Huh," Holly said. "Was that the buzzer?"

Jean was still in another world. "Five letters for 'in line to get, maybe . . .'" She shook her head. "Ugh. The *Times* thinks they're so darn clever."

With a sinking feeling, Holly realized that Jean had not even heard the buzzer. Quickly, she slipped into her room and looked out the window. Amy was already halfway down the block. And — oh, no — some skeevy-looking guy was checking out the flowers! Holly was leaning farther out, getting ready to yell at him, when she realized she couldn't. Not with her mom so close. Thinking quickly, she threw one leg and then the other out the window, landing on the fire escape. She ran down the rickety metal stairs and hit the sidewalk just in time to see the guy walking away, orchid in hand!

"Hey!" she said, running to catch up with him. "Those are my flowers."

"No, they're not," said the guy blandly. "They're mine."

Holly narrowed her eyes. "Is your name Jean?" she asked.

"Huh?" the guy looked confused. Then he recovered. "No, that's my girlfriend's name."

"Oh, yeah," Holly said. She wasn't about to give in. "Then what does the card say?" She put her hands on her hips and waited.

The guy stroked his unshaven chin, thinking. "It says . . . 'happy' — uh—'anniversary. I love you — my sweet — dear — lovely . . .'" He trailed off as Holly reached out and plucked the orchid out of his grasp.

"Get your own flowers!" she said over her shoulder as she dashed back toward her building. Once again, she laid the orchid carefully beneath the buzzer, rang it, and dashed to the fire escape.

Upstairs, she tumbled noisily into her bedroom, recovered, and ran into the living room.

Argh! Her mom wasn't even there! Zoe lay on the floor, still coloring. "Zoe, where's Mom?" she asked, just as the bathroom door opened and Jean stepped back into the room. Holly sighed, exasperated. "Mom, wasn't that the buzzer?" she asked.

"I don't think so," Jean answered calmly. "Are you okay? You're out of breath."

"Oh," Holly said. "Yeah. Aerobics." She started jogging in place, to demonstrate. "Can you believe this school? They even give us homework in gym!" She jogged over to the mirror mounted above the sofa and pretended to catch a glimpse of herself. "Gross!" she cried. "Why didn't you tell me how dirty my hair was? I need a shower! Right now!" Avoiding Jean's wondering eyes, she ran into the bathroom and shut the door, turning the shower on full blast. Then she tiptoed out, ran into her bedroom, and slipped out the window and down the fire escape again.

"Hey!" she shouted, seeing that same skeevy guy walking down the street with her orchid.

He knew he was busted. "What?" he asked. "I was just bringing these to you." He handed them over before she could grab them.

"Thank you," Holly said. She marched to the stoop, placed the flowers, rang the buzzer — for an extra long time, this time — and ran for the fire escape. When she landed in her room, she threw a robe on over her jeans and turbaned a towel around her head. Then she strolled out into the living room.

Jean was just coming in, holding the orchid as if it were loaded. Her eyebrows were knitted in confusion as she stared at it.

"Wow," Holly said, gasping a little. "How beautiful. Who are they for?"

"Me." Jean kept staring at the orchid. "Isn't that weird? Somebody left me flowers."

"Who?" Holly asked, trying to move things along a little.

Jean looked more closely and spotted the card. She pulled it out and read it. Suddenly, she was smiling.

"What's it say?" Holly asked. She could hardly wait to hear Jean say the words.

Jean read it again to herself, then shared it with her daughter. "*How many women can look like a goddess in a bakery uniform?*" she read aloud. "*I couldn't take my eyes off you.*

You are a vision." Her voice cracked a little on the last words. Clearly, she was overcome.

By this time, Zoe had come over to join them. "Who sent them?" she asked.

Jean glanced at the card again, even though she'd already learned every word on it by heart. "*A secret admirer.*" In a daze, she handed the card to Holly. "Who could it be?"

Holly pretended to inspect the card. "Obviously, someone who saw you at the store."

Jean thought for a second. "Yeah," she said, "but how did he know my name?"

Holly didn't even blink. She just pointed to the name tag pinned to Jean's uniform. "Duh," she said helpfully.

"Or — where I live?" Jean asked.

Holly was ready for this one, too. "Hello? *Google.*"

"Maybe he followed you home," Zoe suggested, unhelpfully.

Holly shot her younger sister the stink-eye. That line of thinking was not where she wanted Jean to go.

"Or . . . that I love orchids," Jean said softly, burying her face in the softness of the petals.

"O-R-K-I-D-S," spelled Zoe. "Or is that C-H?" She paused to reflect. "I think it's C-H."

Jean was still wrinkling her forehead. "This is very strange."

"It's scary," Zoe piped up.

Once again, Holly gave her sister the look. Then she turned to her mother. "Mom," she pleaded, "this is the most romantic thing that's ever happened to you in your whole life. Don't judge it. Enjoy it!"

Jean didn't say anything for a moment. Holly crossed her fingers. Then Jean looked up at her daughter. "You're absolutely right," she said, and she walked off to find her vase.

Zoe plucked at the sleeve of Holly's robe. "Why are you wearing jeans underneath your robe?" she asked.

Holly nearly growled at her. "Why do you have bruises all over your body?" She hated to threaten her little sister, but there were times when it was necessary.

Zoe shut her mouth and nodded. She always caught on quickly.

"Wow! You look great!" Holly stared at her mother, her spoonful of cereal halted halfway to her mouth. She put down the spoon and took a good look as Jean walked over to the fridge. Jean's hair was a perfect cascade of ringlets, a beautifully tamed version of the wild mane she'd been sporting since they left Wichita.

Plus, she was smiling.

Plus, she was singing.

She giggled a little. "Amazing what a blow dryer will do when you actually plug it in," she told her daughter. She was gazing at the orchid, which extended gracefully from the vase, transforming the tiny dark kitchen with its simple elegance.

Holly finished her cereal and brought her bowl and Zoe's over to the sink. "I bet you feel great, too," she said to her mom. "Like you're floating on a cloud of infinite possibility."

Jean's eyes widened. "What a beautiful image, Holly." She smiled. "Actually, now that you mention it, that's exactly how I feel. How'd you know that?"

Holly panicked. She'd spouted Ben's line without thinking. "Um," she said, "uh, because I'm your daughter! It's my job to know you." Quickly, before Jean could say another word, she kissed her mother on the cheek, grabbed her books, and took off. "Have a happy day!" she called as she let herself out.

She caught up with Amy in the hall at school, right before math class. "Your uncle's a genius!" she said.

Amy raised her eyebrows. "It worked?"

Holly skipped along happily beside her friend. "She was singing," she reported. "Happy songs. She never sings happy songs."

Amy nodded. "Neither do I," she said. "But don't send me flowers, okay? I like it that way."

But Holly was barely listening. She skipped along to class and headed for an empty seat, passing Adam on the way. He was hunched over, drawing in his sketchbook, as usual. She glanced down at his desk and stopped in her tracks. She couldn't believe what she was seeing! Adam was just adding the final pencil strokes to a drawing of a princess with long, light hair. She sat astride a beautiful, prancing white steed and carried a sword. Lined up behind her were rows and rows of soldiers, clearly in her command.

It was an amazing picture.

But the most amazing thing was that the princess looked exactly like Holly.

"What's that?" Holly asked, once she was able to speak.

Quickly, Adam covered the picture with his arm. "Nothing."

Holly just stood there. "Is that supposed to be me?"

Adam gulped and blushed a little. "No," he said. "That's —
someone else."

Holly was merciless. She reached down and grabbed the
drawing for a closer look. "The face," she said. "It looks
exactly like mine." For some reason, her heart seemed to
be beating extra fast.

A little smile played around the corner of Adam's lips.
"No, it doesn't," he said. He wasn't blushing or hesitating
anymore. "Maybe the face, a little bit. But that woman's on
a horse. You're not on a horse. It's a completely different
person."

Holly couldn't help smiling. She looked at the drawing again,
struck by its power. It really was pretty good. She put it back
down on his desk. "How'd you learn to draw like that?"

"My dad sponsored comic-book conventions when I was
a kid," Adam told her. "He'd take me. Hang around enough,
you pick it up."

Holly nodded. "So, you hung with him a lot, huh?" As

always, when she heard someone talk about a father, she felt slightly jealous.

Adam shook his head, and a cloud seemed to pass over his face. "Uh . . . no," he said. "After he and my mom split, that's about the only thing we did together. But hey, at least I learned to draw, right?"

Now Holly's jealousy was replaced by sympathy. "Divorce as a career builder," she said lightly. "Nice."

They shared a knowing smile.

"You ever been?" Adam asked.

"Divorced?" Holly asked. "Not yet. I plan to be, though."

Adam ignored her joke. "To a comic convention," he said.

"Oh, no," Holly said. "Not that, either."

Adam looked at her, then looked away. "There's one coming up. Six weeks from now. Westside Convention Center. It sounds geeky, but they're fun."

Holly didn't know what to think. Was he inviting her? Just

telling her about it? It was like he had just sort of floated it out there. How was she supposed to respond? For a second, she panicked. This was something she was definitely not used to. This kind of attention — from a boy. Finally, she managed to squeak out a non-answer to his non-invitation. "Yeah," she said, "I'm not much of a planner." She gave him a weird, stiff nod and turned to head for her seat.

Oof!

Holly collided hard with another kid, a guy in glasses.

"Oh," she said as the guy's glasses flew off his face and clattered onto the floor. She bent to pick them up — and so did he. Their heads crashed together with an audible crack. "Ow!" Holly said. She stood up, rubbing her head. "Sorry, sorry," she said, backing away. "Sorry!"

She glanced at Adam and saw that he was trying hard not to laugh. "Please," she begged, "don't draw that."

"I wouldn't dare," Adam said solemnly.

When Jean walked into work that same morning, there was a new bounce to her step. As she worked her way back to the bakery, she scanned the store like a hawk looking for a baby rabbit. Where, oh where, was her secret admirer? She checked out every guy she spotted, wondering if he could be the one. Nobody returned her glance, but that didn't dampen her spirits. "Anyone ask for me?" she asked when she found Gloria and Dolores arranging muffins in the display case.

"Like who?" asked Gloria.

Jean scanned the aisles near the bakery. "I don't know," she said. "Anyone . . ."

Dolores had other things on her mind. "Check this out, Jean," she said, pulling something out of her bag. "This has your name written all over it."

Jean leaned over to see what Dolores was talking about.

Meanwhile, across the store, Lenny the Bread Manager stood watching. He and his assistant, Burt, were going over inventory, but for a moment Lenny let his clipboard fall to his side as he gazed at Jean from afar. He was liking the way she looked, all spruced up. He was convinced her new hairdo had to be a result of his flirting with her the day before. "Do I got juice, or what?" he asked Burt, with a sly grin. "A little attention from me and Jean's poofed up like a peacock."

"It's the guy peacocks who poof up, you know," Burt informed him. Burt was always a stickler for the truth.

Lenny waved off the correction. "You know what I'm saying," he said. "It's an animal thing. She's like a lioness, letting the lion know she's ready." He made a little growling noise, deep in his throat.

Burt couldn't help himself. "It's the guy lions who poof up, too," he muttered.

Fortunately, Jean couldn't hear a word of this ridiculous exchange. She and Gloria were busy looking over the brochure Dolores had pulled out of her purse. "You're crazy," Jean said flatly.

"No, she's not," Gloria said, excited. "You're way too good for this place."

Jean looked again at the brochure. It was a glossy advertisement for a baking contest. She didn't deny that she knew what she was doing when it came to making a cake in the shape of SpongeBob, but this contest was on a whole different level. "But this is a contest for professionals," she said. "I'm basically just a salesperson. And a not-so-good one, at that," she added, thinking of the woman who had stomped off the day before when Jean tried to explain why her idea for a ballerina cake wouldn't work.

Dolores looked at her friend and rolled her eyes. Trying

to remain patient, she said, "Explain something to me. How come when it's a man you're looking at, you're blind to all his flaws, but when it's you, flaws are all you see!"

Jean had to smile at that. Dolores sure did have a point. But just then, someone stuck a long-stemmed yellow rose right in front of her face — and then covered her eyes with a hand so she couldn't see who it was. Her smile grew. It was her secret admirer! "Is it you?" she asked breathlessly.

The hand peeled away from her eyes, and Jean was staring straight at . . . Lenny.

"Yeah, babe," he said in his most studly voice. "It *is* me."

Jean tried not to show her disappointment. Lenny was not exactly her dream man. But — he was a man! And he liked her. She perked up a bit. "I love orchids," she said. "Thank you."

Lenny looked at the rose he was still holding. His forehead wrinkled. "This is a rose," he said.

Jean reached out and took it. "Which I also love," she

said, covering quickly. Either he *wasn't* her secret admirer, or he was, and wasn't ready to reveal himself.

Lenny didn't seem to notice a thing. He grabbed a cookie off a nearby tray and popped it into his mouth. "So," he asked. "You free Saturday night?"

"What'd you have in mind?" Jean asked, looking up at him.

Lenny gave her a superior smile. "Nothing short of rocking your world, babe," he answered.

Jean looked doubtful. "My world doesn't rock all that easily," she said.

Dolores, passing by with a tray of muffins, snorted. "That's right, girlfriend," she said. "Make him work for it!"

Lenny leaned in toward Jean, still chewing on his cookie. "That's on account of your world not being rocked yet by Lenny 'The World Rocker' Horton," he said suavely.

Jean still looked doubtful. "Let's say after I check my social calendar, it turns out I am free Saturday night. Where are we going?"

Lenny leaned back, ready to clinch the deal. "Only to hear the greatest American band ever to pipe out a power ballad," he announced. "To a Styx concert!"

If he was looking for a big response, he didn't get one from Jean. Her tastes ran more to jazz and world music than to heavy metal. But she tried to fake a certain excitement. "Something I've never done!" she said brightly.

Lenny knew he had her on the line. It was time to reel her in. "Ooh," he said, "a Styx newbie! Darn, I must really like you. Talk about hot tickets!" He strolled off, strumming air guitar as he made his way back to his lair, the bread shelves.

10

Saturday night, Jean was putting the final touches on her makeup while Holly watched. It had been quite a while since she'd seen her mom in anything but jeans or a uniform. Holly was trying to enjoy the sight of her mother in a dress, looking so happy and pretty, but she couldn't help worrying. Jean had decided Lenny was her secret admirer, and nothing Holly said was changing her mind. "How many times do I have to tell you?" she tried one more time. "It's *impossible* that Lenny is your secret admirer!"

Jean pursed her lips and traced them with a lip pencil. "Nothing's impossible," she said calmly.

"No," Holly argued. "Some things *are*. Like a man who gives a woman an orchid — the most romantic flower — also giving her a yellow rose, which is" — she remembered what Ben had said — "what you send to your sick grandmother in the hospital!"

Jean finished applying her lipstick, tucked it into her purse, and left the bathroom. Holly followed her.

In Jean's room, Zoe was sitting on the bed, trying on every single piece of Jean's jewelry. She was draped in necklaces and stuck all over with brooches. Just as she was putting on a pile of bangles, the doorbell rang. "I'll get it!" she squealed, running off with a loud jingle.

Holly watched as Jean took one last look in the full-length mirror. She couldn't let it go. "I read the note," she told her mom. "A guy like that — a poet — doesn't take a woman to a Styx concert." She conveniently forgot to mention the fact that she had *written* the note.

"Well, it's different," said Jean, who wasn't all that thrilled about the concert, but was trying to make the best of it.

"So is a peanut butter and glue sandwich," Holly cried in exasperation. "That doesn't mean you eat it!"

Jean stopped looking into the mirror. She turned to face her daughter. "Holly," she said seriously, "I like this guy, and he seems to like me. Would it kill you to give him a chance?" With that, she swept out into the living room to greet Lenny.

Zoe was leading Lenny into the apartment, having introduced herself at the door. "Princess Zoe?" Lenny was asking, a little awkwardly.

"Yes," Zoe insisted. "You can tell I'm a princess from all my necklaces." She spelled it out for him. "N-E-C-K-L-A-C-E-S."

Lenny nodded, though Holly, watching, could tell that he totally didn't get it. "Yeah," he said. "Okay. That makes sense."

He turned to look at Jean. "Whoa!" he cried. "Where'd you get the outfit? White-hot-dot-com?"

Holly didn't bother to hide her disgust. She sighed and rolled her eyes.

Clueless, Lenny took out his wallet, opened it, and took out a twenty. "Your mom told me Saturdays are movie nights for you guys, so here, on me, take your sister to see *Bambi*." He thrust the money at Holly.

She didn't take it. "Not sure *Bambi*'s actually in theaters now," she informed him, "what with it coming out, oh, fifty years ago. Which is a shame," she added snidely, "'cause it sure would be fun to take my seven-year-old sister to a story where the mom gets killed by an evil male hunter."

Zoe perked up. "I want to see that!" she said.

Jean took the money from Lenny's hand and put it into Holly's. "Thank you, Lenny," she said in a teacherly voice. "That's very nice of you." She glared at Holly.

"Thank you, Lenny," Holly finally choked out the words.

With one more glare at Holly, Jean let Lenny usher her out the door. As they left, Holly plopped down on the couch. "M-O-R-O-N," she spelled.

"Moo-ron?" Zoe guessed. "What does that mean?"

Holly just shook her head. "Forget it," she said.

Downstairs, Lenny was opening the passenger door of his car, a shiny Camaro from the late sixties. He touched it so tenderly that Jean could tell right away how much the car meant to him. "Wow," she said. "What a pretty car."

Lenny preened a little. "Rebuilt everything. Even the tranny." He watched as she got ready to climb in. "Uh," he said, "in fact, I just got new mats, so do you mind taking your shoes off?"

Holly and Zoe were watching from the window upstairs as Jean pulled off one shoe, then the other. That did it. Holly headed for the phone and dialed.

Amy answered on the second ring. "Let me guess," she said as soon as she heard Holly's voice. "The sick-grandma argument didn't fly?"

"She barely heard it," Holly said disgustedly. "She was too busy visualizing her future as Mrs. Lenny Hair Band. He has to be derailed."

"By what?" Amy wanted to know.

Holly didn't have a clue. "I don't know," she admitted. But she knew who *would* know. "Tell you what. I'm gonna drop Zoe off at Dolores's. Meet me at the bistro in twenty."

"Ice cream's gonna help?" Amy asked.

"No!" said Holly. "Your uncle will. He knew about the orchids, right? He'll know what to do next."

Jean was a little surprised when Lenny pulled up to a small roadhouse out on the highway. Would Styx really be playing at a place this size? But when she walked in with him, she realized they had to be in the right place.

Everyone in the bar looked like they'd walked straight out of the eighties. She hadn't seen so many mullets and so much bad acid wash since Ronald Reagan was in office. She followed Lenny through the crowd until they landed at the bar, next to an overweight guy with one or two teeth and long, ratty hair. Jean looked away, but Lenny grinned at the guy.

"The Len Man!" said the toothless rocker. "Wassup, brother?"

"Just rocking out, Squonk," Lenny reported, giving his friend a ten-step soul shake that ended with them linking pinkies and fluttering their fingers like butterflies. Then they cracked up and slapped each other five.

Jean looked on, mystified. Just then, the lights went down and three power chords echoed through the club. The crowd went wild.

"ARE YOU READY TO ROCK?" shouted an announcer.

The crowd went berserk.

"ARE YOU READY FOR THE GREATEST ROCK AND ROLL BAND OF ALL TIME?"

The crowd lost its mind.

"THEN PUT YOUR HANDS TOGETHER FOR . . . almost . . . STYX!!!!"

With that, the lights went up and the band hit the stage.

Jean stared. These guys were in their twenties! They were nowhere *near* old enough to be Styx. They pranced about onstage, whipping their hair around. Inwardly, Jean groaned.

A tribute band.

The lead singer grabbed the mic and the band tore into "Mr. Roboto." The crowd started cheering like crazy as soon as they heard the opening notes. Next to Jean, Lenny was wailing on his air guitar.

"Uh, Lenny?" Jean interrupted his dramatics. "I haven't really kept up with Styx, but that doesn't look anything like their singer."

Lenny was oblivious. Now he was playing air drums, furiously whipping his nonexistent hair.

"Len?" Jean asked, watching as Lenny switched to air bass. "I don't think that's Styx." She was beginning to wonder if he even knew the difference.

Lenny had started dancing. He turned to her. "They're better than Styx!" he shouted. "They're known as Killroy, a tribute to Styx. Close your eyes," he commanded. "You can't even tell the difference." He reached out and put his hands over her eyes.

The lead singer reached for a high note, and his voice cracked and went flat.

"No," Jean said, realizing it was hopeless to argue. "You can't tell."

Things were hopping at the River Bistro. It was a whole different scene on a Saturday night. The tables were full of well-dressed customers, the wine was flowing, and the noise level was high.

Ben was behind the counter in the open kitchen, doing a dozen things at once. He glanced up as Holly and Amy approached.

"We have a question," Amy said, marching right up to the counter.

"Girls," Ben said, "I'm busy. Can it wait?" He turned to stop a waiter who was trying to sneak out without displaying a plate of food for inspection.

"It's important!" Holly said urgently.

Amy tried an approach she knew would work with her uncle. "It's for a school paper," she said. "Due tomorrow!"

Ben looked skeptical.

Holly jumped in. "We wanted to know what the perfect man would do as a follow-up to orchids."

Ben sighed. "Not now," he said, sprinkling some parsley over a filet of salmon. "Let's talk tomorrow."

Just then, the bartender passed by. Lance was all ears when it came to perfect men. "What can be more important than the perfect man?" he asked.

"Lance . . ." Ben said, his voice a warning. Once they got Lance on their side, the girls would win and he knew it.

"Don't 'Lance' me," Lance said haughtily. "You take a break and help these girls. Try the new red wine, sit at your table, and let me handle things."

"But —" Ben tried to protest.

"Shhh," Lance told him, putting a glass of wine into his hand. Reluctantly, Ben followed the girls over to a corner table and they all sat down.

"So," Ben said, "what is this? A school paper on dating? For what class?"

"English," Holly said quickly. "I'm — well, I'm looking at romantic heroes in literature, like — like —"

Amy saw that her friend was floundering. "Romeo," she suggested.

"Right!" said Holly, relieved. "And Heathcliff! Guys like that. I'm comparing them to their real-life counterparts." That sounded good, didn't it?

But Ben wasn't buying it. "I thought you didn't believe in romance," he reminded her.

Holly shrugged. "I'm trying to stretch."

Ben sighed. "I'm not exactly an authority on this."

Just then, there was a loud crashing sound from the kitchen. Ben shot up and stared at Lance, who looked back, full of guilt.

"Bad plate," Lance said. "Bad!"

Ben slumped back in his seat, rolled his eyes, and gave up. Smiling, Holly whipped out a tape recorder and turned it on. "So," she asked, speaking into the mic, "what makes today's perfect man perfect? What exactly is it he says, or does, that makes him a woman's perfect man?"

Ben considered this. "That depends," he said at last. "Every woman's different."

"But," Holly said, confused, "orchids work for all of them?"

"Sure," Ben said. "As a gesture. But that's just a starting point. For a man to be perfect for a woman, he has to be more connected to her than that. He has to know what makes her tick." He frowned, frustrated. "That's why, without knowing what woman you're talking about, it's kind of a moot point —"

Holly interrupted him. It was time for more information. "She listens to Patsy Cline when she's sad." Then she realized she might be giving too much away, and backtracked. "Hypothetically," she added, toying with the spoon at her place setting. "*Say* she does. What then?"

Ben nodded. He liked specifics, even if they were hypothetical. "Is she sad a lot?" he asked.

"Yes," Holly answered. "Too much."

"Okay," Ben said. "Well, he absolutely can't be one of those guys who are afraid of tears."

*   *   *

At that very moment, back at the roadhouse, Lenny was weeping. The Styx tribute band was moving their audience with the song "Babe," Lenny included. He was standing on a chair, holding up a glow-stick. He put his arm around Jean, and she looked up at him. Tears were streaming down Lenny's cheeks as he lip-synched along with the singer.

"'Because it's you, babe,'" he sang, looking deep into Jean's eyes, "'giving me the courage and the strength I need, please believe that it's true — babe, I love you!'" He stopped singing and gave Jean an even more intense look. "It's like he wrote it about us," he told her.

At the bistro, the girls were still listening to every word Ben had to say. ". . . And he has to know how to cheer her up," he was telling them. "Let's see. If Patsy's her sad music . . ." He thought about it for a moment, then he hopped up to fetch a CD from his collection behind the bar. "This is the music that will make her happy," he said, handing it to Holly.

She looked at the CD. He'd obviously burned it himself.

"Keep it," Ben said.

Holly thanked him as she tucked it away. Then she decided to go for it and ask one more question. "What if she's into word games," she asked. "Scrabble, stuff like that?"

Ben smiled. "Then she's smart. She'll need a man who likes that stuff, too," he said, as if it were obvious. "A little wit, a little wordplay."

Holly was liking these answers. "Okay," she said. "But — how about if she's been dumped a lot? What then?"

Ben frowned and thought that over. Holly and Amy leaned in, waiting to hear his answer. Finally, he said, "For a woman who's seen some heartbreak — for any woman, really — the perfect guy is the one who could be anywhere in the world and chooses to be with her because life is better with her by his side." That speech delivered, he leaned back in his seat — just as the door opened and a stunning blond woman walked over to their table.

Heads turned all through the restaurant as she saun-tered by. She was a knockout. Amy leaned over to Holly. "That's Amber," she whispered.

Amber didn't even say hello. "Big problem," she said to Ben. "Vera Wang, bias cut, *heaven*. It's wedding chic." She leaned over to give Amy a kiss on the cheek. "Hey, cutie," she said.

"Hi, Amber," Amy said.

"Where's the problem?" Ben asked.

"It's a small fortune," Amber answered. "No, that's a lie. It's a large fortune."

Ben didn't hesitate. "It's your day," he said. "Do it."

Amber broke into a huge smile. Holly could see how relieved she was. "I adore you," Amber told Ben. "Now, what about the bridesmaids?"

Ben held up his hands. "Hello?" he asked. "I *work* here. I'm trying to run a business."

Amber ignored him. Reaching out for his hands, she

pulled him to his feet and walked off with him. "I'm thinking chiffon . . ." she began as they disappeared.

"Wow," Holly said, watching her go. "She's gorgeous."

Amy nodded. "Yup. Together, they look like the winners of the genetic lottery."

Holly realized that her interview was over. She clicked off the tape recorder and sat for a moment gazing down at the cover of the CD.

Later that night, *much* later, Holly watched out the window as Lenny's Camaro pulled up to the curb in front of their building. He got out and came around to open the door for Jean. When she got out — shoeless — she said, "Thank you, Lenny. That was —"

Before she could finish, Lenny filled in the blank. "I know," he said. "You're good times, Jean. I could get used to this." He leaned in for a quick kiss. Then he gave Jean a wink and pointed his finger at her. He jumped back into his car and peeled out, tearing off down the street.

When Jean came in, Holly was sitting in the living room. "So," she said. "How was the eighties flashback?"

Jean jumped. She hadn't expected Holly to wait up for her. "My God!" she yelped. "You scared me."

"His stupid car is louder than a jumbo jet," Holly explained. "Probably woke up the whole neighborhood."

Jean came to sit down with her daughter. "Holly, for me, will you give Lenny a chance?"

"Mom," Holly answered instantly, "for me, will you go slow this time? You don't know who else is out there."

"No," Jean admitted tiredly. "But here's what I do know. Tonight, I had a pretty good time."

Holly gave up. Pulling her robe around her, she got up to head back to bed. "Then you have bigger problems than I ever imagined," she said over her shoulder as she left the room.

11

That Monday, Amy and Holly sat next to each other in English class. Mr. Orbach was lecturing, but Holly wasn't exactly listening. Her mind was on much more important matters.

"'O, what a tangled web we weave,'" Mr. Orbach was quoting, "'when first we practice to deceive.'" He looked around the room. "Who wants to talk about what that means?" Some hands went up. Holly took the opportunity to lean over to Amy.

"He needs to write her a letter," she whispered urgently.

"Who?" Amy asked.

"The perfect man."

At that moment, Mr. Orbach looked at Adam, whose hand did not happen to be raised. "Adam," he said. "Care to elucidate us?"

Adam looked up, surprised. He wasn't big on talking in class.

"Yes, you," Mr. Orbach said. "What do you think Sir Walter Scott was saying?"

Amy stared at Holly. "You're going to forge a letter?" she hissed.

"I have to," Holly whispered back. "If I don't, my mom's going to be walking up the aisle to the sound of 'Wheel in the Sky.'"

Adam was trying to find a reasonable answer for Mr. Orbach. "Um, I think — I think it's that lies get complicated," he said.

"Because?" Mr. Orbach prompted.

Adam looked down at his hands. "Because, um," he stumbled, "usually if you lie once, you have to lie again."

Holly would have liked to hear what Adam was saying, but she was too busy whispering to Amy. "Except," she said, thinking as she whispered, "she'll recognize my handwriting."

Amy smiled slyly. "She won't recognize mine," she suggested.

"Until," Adam was still talking, on a roll now, "eventually, all you have is a big mass of lies that you can't find your way out of. . . ."

Holly liked Amy's answer. "Does it look like adult handwriting?" she asked.

"Hello," Amy answered, "who do you think signs my report cards?"

"So, basically," Adam finished, "I think maybe his point is that things go better when everyone just tells the truth."

Holly smiled at Amy. "We'll do it right after school," she said.

Amy smiled at Holly. "Perfect."

* * *

That afternoon, Holly lay on Amy's bed, checking out the Pink Martini CD Ben had given her. Amy came in, carrying some nice-looking stationery she'd swiped from her mom. "Got it," she said, waving the linen paper. She settled down to write.

Holly turned on the tape recorder, and her own voice floated into the room. "What if she's into word games — Scrabble, stuff like that?"

"Then she's smart," Ben's voice answered. "She'll need a man who likes that stuff, too. A little wit, a little word-play . . ."

"Wit," Holly said.

Amy nodded, pen poised. "And wordplay."

An hour later, Holly dropped a fat envelope into a mailbox as she headed home. "I know what I'm doing borders on delusional," she said, although there was nobody there to hear her, "but trust me — if you met Lenny, you'd do the same."

That night, she worked on her blog.

username: GIRL ON THE MOVE

I'm listening to: There is no music for how I feel.

current mood: nervous

The truth is, I'm tired. Of bubble wrap and change-of-address cards. Of figuring out new towns and making new friends. It's not fun anymore. It's just not.

In school the next day, Holly found herself alone at lunchtime. She wandered through the cafeteria with her tray, trying to figure out where she could sit. Without quite meaning to, she strolled by a table where Adam was sitting by himself. He was, as usual, drawing. Holly got a glimpse. It was the princess again, the princess with Holly's face.

"I thought I told you not to draw me," she said.

He looked up and saw her. "I thought I told you it wasn't you," he answered right back.

Holly held his glance. Then she looked down at the picture. This time, the princess was all alone in a field. "Where'd her troops go?" she asked.

"She needed a little quiet time," Adam answered. "To think things through."

"What kind of things?" Holly asked, curious. She put down her tray.

"Like what her next step is," Adam said. "Whether she's going to form an alliance with a prince, or go it alone." He wasn't quite meeting her eyes now.

"What's she gonna choose?" Holly asked, playing along.

Adam smiled. "I think she's going to go for the prince."

"Really?"

"Yeah," Adam said. "He's kind of a great guy. He's handsome. He's nice."

"He can draw," Holly added.

Adam ducked that one. "Actually, he can't. But he's very good at archery, and — that thing with the pole."

"Jousting?" Holly had forgotten all about her lunch by now.

"Yes," Adam said, clearly loving this game. "You should see him joust. He's like Joe Jouster. Any time you want to hang out with him, he's like, 'I can't hang out. I have to practice my jousting.'"

Holly cracked up.

Adam laughed, too. "You want to sit down?" he asked when he'd caught his breath.

Holly looked at the chair next to Adam's. She *absolutely* wanted to sit down. But — she was also terrified of how much she wanted to. "I, um, I made plans with . . . someone," she stuttered lamely.

Adam's smile faded. "I thought you weren't much of a planner," he reminded her.

"Oh. Yeah." Holly wanted to disappear. "I'll see you," she said finally, picking up her tray and backing away.

That night, Holly was giving Zoe a bath. "Holly," Zoe asked as she zoomed her devil duck all around the tub, "do you think we're going to stay here?"

"I don't know," Holly said. She scooped up some suds and soaped Zoe's shoulders. "Why?"

Zoe looked up at her through wet bangs. "There's a big spelling bee coming up with all the other schools," she told her sister. "My teacher entered me."

Holly sat back on her heels. "I bet you'll win! You're the best speller I ever met."

"Yeah," Zoe agreed. "Only it's not for a couple of months."

"Oh." Holly knew how *that* felt.

"Yeah." Zoe did, too.

"Maybe we'll still be here," Holly said, picking up another handful of suds.

Zoe sighed. "I hope so. I've never entered anything."

Holly heard the front door open, and in a moment Jean came in, holding a big envelope. She looked as if she were in shock.

"Mommy?" Zoe asked. "Are you sick?"

Jean didn't seem to hear her. "What?"

"You don't look normal," Zoe observed.

"I got a letter," Jean said, zombielike.

Holly tried to look surprised and innocent and interested. "What kind?"

"It's — it's a love letter," Jean said, still looking as if she were sleepwalking. "Somebody wrote me a love letter." She walked out of the bathroom, still holding the envelope.

Holly helped Zoe out of the bath. The two girls followed

their mother into the living room. "What's it say?" Zoe asked.

Jean couldn't even answer. She just handed the letter to Holly.

Holly opened it. There, in Amy's handwriting, was the letter. "*My dearest Jean,*" she read aloud. "*The letters J-E-A-N used to spell out just another word for denim. But since I found you, I hear those four letters and all I can think of is another four-letter word.*" Holly paused for effect. "*L-O-V-E,*" she went on.

"Love?" Zoe asked.

"Right," Jean answered.

"He loves you?" Zoe asked.

Jean nodded dreamily. "That's what he says."

"Ugh!" Zoe made a horrible face, as if love were brussels sprouts.

But Holly hadn't finished yet. "*Being near you is like standing on a triple word score. . . .*"

"He plays Scrabble," Jean breathed.

"*Everything matters three times as much,*" Holly continued. "*The sun shines three times as brightly. The birds sing three times as loudly. And I'm three times as happy.*" Holly poked inside the envelope and pulled out a CD. "What's this?" she asked.

"He gave you a present!" Zoe squealed. "I like him now."

Holly went over to the boom box to put the CD on.

Jean was still sitting there, dazed. "Smart," she said. "Witty, romantic . . ."

Holly turned to face her mother. "Please tell me you don't still think it's Lenny!"

Jean nodded. "It *is* kind of hard to picture Lenny playing Scrabble," she admitted.

Then the music kicked in. It was Pink Martini singing "Sympathique." The beat was happy, infectious. Jean jumped up, grabbed Zoe's hands, and started dancing around the room. Holly watched, thinking how incredibly smart Ben must be. This music really *did* make her mother happy. Well, the music — and the letter.

Jean came over and grabbed Holly, pulling her into the circle, and all three Hamilton girls danced wildly to the happy, happy beat.

"And he sent you a present, too?" During break time at the A&P, Jean was filling Gloria in on everything that had happened.

Jean glanced down Aisle Five. Lenny grinned back at her, juggling four cans of soup in a very show-offy way. She smiled back at him, but her smile was forced. She was beginning to believe that Holly was right: No way was Lenny her secret admirer.

Jean turned back to face Gloria, who was holding the letter. "Yeah, he also sent me a CD. A band I never heard of, but I *loved*. It's like he knows me better than I know myself."

"So why's he hiding?" Gloria asked.

Jean was taken aback. "He's not *hiding*," she said. "He's just —" She paused, trying to think.

"Just what?" Gloria asked.

Jean searched her mind desperately, but no answer came. She was relieved when Dolores spoke up.

"Good *lord*," Dolores said, from behind them. "Someone's got a little extra inspiration today!"

Jean and Gloria turned around. Dolores was staring down at a cake on the counter. No, it was more than a cake. It was a fairy tale come to life. The cake itself was a sailboat, sailing on a placid lake of blue candy. Dotted on the shore were picturesque huts made of chocolate and marshmallow.

Jean shrugged, blushing a little. "I'm in a romantic mood," she said. "I guess it shows."

"I *guess*," Dolores echoed. She pulled a Polaroid camera out of a drawer and started taking pictures of the cake. While she waited for them to develop, she put the camera back — and noticed the contest brochure stuffed in the back of the drawer. "Hey," she said to Jean. "I thought you sent this in."

"Oh," said Jean. Busted. "No. Not yet."

Gloria couldn't believe it. "What are you waiting for?" she asked. "If you win this thing, you could end up working in a fancy French bakery in the city."

Jean shook her head. "I can't win a contest like that," she said.

Dolores stood up straight. Her eyes flashed. "Can't?" she roared. "Did I hear right? Did she say *can't?*"

"That's what I heard," Gloria said.

Dolores wiped her hands on a towel. She shook her head. And she headed off to the mixer, sighing. "Oh, no, no, no," she muttered. "I don't listen to 'can't.' I don't understand 'can't.' I listen to 'can' and 'do' and 'will.'" She looked back at Jean. "You come back to me when you got yourself a new vocabulary."

Jean and Gloria looked at each other, shrugged, and smiled. Then Gloria picked up the brochure and shoved it into Jean's hand.

Later that night, Jean showed the brochure to Zoe and Holly. They sat at the kitchen table reading it while Jean stood by the counter, icing a cake. Jean did not look happy. She frowned as she spread the thick, gooey frosting. Then she shook her head. "There must be something wrong with him," she said.

"Who?" Zoe asked, eyeing the frosting-covered spatula in her mother's hand.

"Mr. Wonderful," Jean answered.

"What?" Holly asked, alarmed. "There's nothing wrong with him! He's perfect!"

Jean frowned. "Then why all the secrecy? Why not just come up to me, show his face, and say hello? Like a normal person."

Holly realized it was time for some serious damage control. "Listen to yourself," she said. "A guy's the least bit romantic, and suddenly you decide he's not normal."

But Jean was on a roll. "How do I know if he is? And if he is, what does he look like?" She closed her eyes, as if trying to picture him. "Is he tall? Short? Does he dress formal? T-shirts and jeans? Curly blond hair, straight black hair? What?"

Holly was at a loss for words. "I'm sure he's very handsome," she managed to say.

Jean turned to face her. "How do you know?" she asked.

Yikes. Gulp. "'Cause he writes like he's handsome," Holly said, knowing it sounded lame.

Jean laughed. "Honey, have you seen pictures of Shakespeare? Bald. Skinny."

Holly sighed. "What does it matter, anyway?"

Jean had an answer. "Because you can't have a relationship with a man you've never laid eyes on."

* * *

"Got it," Amy said the next day at school as she walked up to Holly's locker. She handed over a digital camera.

"Thanks!" Holly said. Taking the camera, she headed down the hall, with Amy behind her.

Amy trotted to catch up. "Um, not to be the dull voice of reason or anything, but have you thought about how you're going to end this?"

Holly hadn't. "I'll think of something," she said.

"Because this is starting to feel funky," Amy told her.

"No," Holly corrected her friend. "Watching my mom spiral downward after a breakup, having to remind her to eat — *that* feels funky. Seeing her smile feels *good*."

Amy saw Holly's point. But, still. "I just mean —"

"Amy." Holly stopped dead in the middle of the hall. "She's thinking of entering a cake contest."

Amy looked bewildered. "I'm sure that means something to somebody," she said.

Holly nodded. "It means that having the perfect man in her life is making my mom care about herself — maybe for the first time ever." She grabbed Amy's hand. "C'mon, we've got work to do."

Amy and Holly spent most of their free time at school racing around with the camera, hoping to find Mr. Perfect. They took shots of every guy who *might* work, but as they looked closer, they realized this search was going to be harder than they thought.

The hunky Spanish teacher was too young.

The science teacher was way, *way* too old.

The gym teacher was buff, and his tight shorts were a plus, but then he screamed at some kids and blew his whistle. When they looked at Amy's picture, they could see the veins in his neck sticking out. Too angry.

After school, they headed for the streets. Holly spotted the most gorgeous guy she'd ever seen, waiting to cross the street. "Perfect," she whispered to Amy. "Ask him if we can take his picture."

"No," Amy whispered back. "He could say no. I'll just sneak one." She lifted the viewfinder to her eye, just in time to catch the guy as he started to pick his nose. He was really going for it. Amy lowered the camera.

"Found one!" said Amy, a little later. She took a picture and showed it to Holly. It was of a guy in a chicken costume.

"That's not funny," Holly said.

Amy tried again with a picture of an extremely good-looking thirteen-year-old.

"That's not funny," Holly said again.

Then there was the totally normal-looking guy who slipped off his shirt to show off a chest completely covered in tattoos. There were a few interesting piercings, too.

"Okay," Holly admitted. "That one's kind of funny."

By the end of the afternoon, both girls were totally

A monthly mixer for single parents?! Holly cringes with shame at the dating suggestions her mom offers at the high school's parent-and-student night.

After reading a romantic letter sent by Jean's secret admirer, the Hamilton girls dance to the happy, infectious beat of the music he sent.

"*D*id it hurt when you fell from heaven?" Holly isn't as impressed as her mother is by Lenny's cheesy pickup lines.

Daydreaming about the perfect man, who is a great cook and loves to play Scrabble, just like Jean. Too good to be true?

"Ben? As in *Ben* Ben?" Jean is shocked to receive a call from her dream date. But is he really calling from China?

*F*inally! Holly kisses Adam back for the first time — and it's just like a real first kiss should be!

Holly takes Ben on a walk by her mom's new workplace. "That's her," says Holly. Now Ben can finally put a face to Jean's name.

bummed. "This is hopeless," Holly said as they sat on a bench in Prospect Park.

Amy wasn't quite ready to give up. She pointed out a short, nearly bald man. "Him?"

Holly snorted. "Smeagol, from *The Lord of the Rings?*" She went into an excellent impression of the character. "Does my precious want to go see a movie with Smeagol? My precious!"

Amy cracked up. "Now I know why your mom can't find the right guy. *You're* too picky."

Holly ignored her. She was still scanning the people walking by. Then she spotted a flower cart. "Wait!" she said suddenly. "I know who could play the perfect man."

"Who?" Amy asked. Then she followed Holly's glance, saw the flowers, and realized what her friend meant. "Yes!"

The girls ran all the way to the River Bistro.

Ben seemed to wince when he saw them walk in. "Honey,"

he said to his niece, "I got a party of fifty coming in half an hour."

"It'll only take a second," Holly assured him.

Lance spoke up from behind the bar. "You can take my picture! Just shoot it from my good side — my right side. From the right, I look like Brad Pitt. From the left, I look like David Spade."

Ben gave Lance a dirty look. "Hey, you're busy, too. We're missing a setup here!" He pointed to a half-set table. Ben turned to Holly and Amy. "Look, I'm sorry," he said. "We're swamped."

Amy wasn't daunted. "Hey, Uncle Ben," she said. "What's that stuff you put on top of your spinach salad? Parmesan *what*?"

Ben looked up. "Cheese."

Click.

Amy shot the picture.

* * *

The girls went back to Amy's and got busy. And that very night, Jean had another letter — and a picture. She stared down at Ben's smiling face as Holly and Zoe leaned over her shoulder. "Ben," she said musingly. "That's a nice name. Uncomplicated. Dependable. Ben."

Holly couldn't resist. "It beats Lenny, that's for sure. Plus, he's cuter."

"Don't you be mean about Lenny," Jean told her. "He's a good egg. Just not the egg for me."

Zoe grabbed Ben's picture and hugged it tight. "I like this egg," she said. "I want this egg to be my boyfriend. When's he coming over?"

Jean read the letter again. "As soon as he comes back, he says."

"Oh?" Holly pretended to be clueless. "Where'd he go?"

"He's opening up a new restaurant in China," Jean reported. "The phones there are impossible, evidently, but as soon as he's back he's going to call."

Holly smiled to herself. It was working! Jean bought the whole thing. "What else did he say?" she asked, leaning in to look.

Jean held the letter to her chest so Holly couldn't see it. "It's private," she said. Private — and beautiful. Jean had made up her mind. Ben was the man for her.

13

She had to let him down easy. Jean wasn't used to breaking up with guys. In fact, she couldn't remember if she'd ever done it before. Usually she was the one who got dumped.

It was time. Lenny was standing there, right in front of her. Jean fidgeted with her apron strings. "Lenny," she began, "I need to tell you something."

"Shhh," Lenny said, putting a finger to his lips and winking at her. "We don't need words. I know what you're gonna say, and I feel the exact same way."

Jean gulped, but tried to forge on. "No, it's important that I say this. I met someone, and —"

Again, Lenny interrupted her. "And his name is Lenny. And

he's rocking my world. I know. And I know you're scared. I'm scared, too." Then he began quoting a Styx song. "'But I know if the world turned upside down, baby, I know, you'd always be on my mind.'"

Ouch. Jean waited patiently for him to finish. Then she went on. "I met someone else," she said firmly. "I mean, I didn't meet someone, but I might. One day, that is. And when I do, I don't want to be going out with you. Sorry."

Lenny stood back. "Whoa, baby, whoa!" He shook his head. "You're freakin' with my mind here. What are you talking about? You want to break up because you *might* meet someone else?"

Jean nodded. "Kind of. Yeah."

Lenny could not believe his ears. "But the perfect man is standing right here, next to my cuddles."

Cuddles? Jean cleared her throat. "I'm sorry, Lenny. I really am. You're a good man." Lenny looked so devastated that Jean could only think of one thing to do. She began to hum a Styx song that she knew he loved.

Lenny managed a weak smile, and Jean knew he was going to survive.

Meanwhile, Amy and Holly were plotting in the school cafeteria. "China?" Amy asked. "How are we going to get a stamp from China?"

"We won't," Holly said simply. "Now that he's 'traveling,' he asked her to send her e-mail address to his e-mail address."

Amy blinked. "He has an e-mail address?"

"BrooklynBoy." Holly caught Amy's look. "It's a new account I'm about to set up."

Amy shook her head. "And it's consistent, since everyone lies in cyberspace."

Now Holly came to the problem. "Except we can't use my computer in case my mom finds it."

Amy didn't have a solution. "I'd offer ours, but my brother's on it twenty-four/seven buying Yu-Gi-Oh cards on eBay."

"Who else?" Holly and Amy looked around the crowded, noisy cafeteria. Way over on the other side, Adam sat alone, hunched over his sketchbook.

"It's kind of messy," Adam said, after school that day, as he led Holly into his room. The walls were covered with classic comics and fantasy art of unicorns and dragons. The windows were covered with tapestries in dark colors. A computer glowed on the cluttered desk.

"It's kind of — *dark*," Holly said, looking around.

"Oh," said Adam. "Yeah." He walked over to the window and yanked down the tapestry covering it. He balled it up and tossed it behind him. As he did, he looked down to see a picture on the floor. One of his sketches featuring

Holly. Quickly, he stepped on it so she wouldn't see. He pointed to the desk. "Help yourself," he said.

When Holly sat down, Adam sidled over to his bed and stuck the picture under his pillow.

Holly waited for the system to sign on. "Thanks so much for letting me do this," she said. "I know it probably seems crazy to you. But at least my mom is happy. Which is a change. She usually spends a lot of time, you know, depressed. Or with idiots."

Adam nodded in recognition. "Maybe I should try it. My mother only smiles once a month, when her alimony check comes."

Holly reached over to press PLAY on her tape recorder. "How about if she's been dumped a lot?" her own voice drifted out. "What then?"

Adam settled in on his bed with a copy of *Optic Nerve*. Was he reading? Or just pretending to read as he watched Holly?

Ben's voice filled the room. "For a woman who's seen some heartbreak — for any woman, really — the perfect guy is the one who could be anywhere in the world and chooses to be with her because life is better with her by his side."

Holly thought for a moment. Then she started typing.

That night, Holly pretended to concentrate on painting Zoe's toenails as she secretly watched Jean sign on and read her mail. She knew exactly what Jean was seeing on the screen, but it still gave her chills up her spine when her mom read it out loud.

"Unbelievable," Jean said. "Listen to this." She leaned toward the computer screen. "*I'm spending my days with very serious businesspeople*," she read, "*and I know I should be listening to every word they say, but all I keep thinking is, what am I doing all the way in China? I planned this restaurant before I ever laid eyes on you. If I had it to do over, I'd buy the building right next to yours and open there."*

Jean stopped reading and put her hand over her heart. She looked over at Holly, and Holly could see the tears glistening in her eyes. "He'd rather be with me," Jean whispered.

14

Over the next few days, things really began to heat up — and not just between Jean and Mr. Perfect.

Holly noticed it the next time she went over to Adam's to use his computer. He was lying on the floor — drawing, of course — as she worked at his desk. Every time she stole a look at him, she caught him looking back at her. She'd smile a little, then go back to her work. She was reading a note from Passionate Baker to BrooklynBoy.

Dear BrooklynBoy, it said, **If your food's half as good as your letters, nothing would make me happier than having your restaurant on my block. But I'd hate to deprive the nation of China**

of that kind of satisfaction. So open your restaurant there first.

Wow! Jean sounded so witty and happy. Holly was so involved with what she was reading that she didn't even notice when Adam grabbed his webcam and stole a shot of her at the computer.

Holly kept reading to herself. **It's a real specific kind of satisfaction, isn't it?** Jean had written. **Cooking for people. I'm only a baker, but I put as much creativity and passion into my cakes as a painter puts on a canvas. Granted, when all's said and done, all I've made is a cake. But then again, you can't eat the Mona Lisa.**

"Whew!" Holly said out loud. "Nicely said, Mom." She noted Jean's sign-off: **Waiting — Passionate Baker**, and realized she had some work to do. Leaning over the keyboard, she began to type.

Dear Passionate Baker, she wrote, imagining the

voice of the perfect man. **Creativity and passion, huh? I'm starting to figure out what makes you tick. . . .** Holly thought some more, snuck some more glances at Adam, and wrote some more. **And as for the Mona Lisa, after a few thousand years, people will get tired of her smile, but a good fudge brownie is eternal.**

Jean couldn't believe what she was reading. That night, as she worked on yet another fairy-tale cake, she kept dashing back and forth to her computer to carry on her "conversation" with Mr. Perfect. First she would add a turret of caramel lace to her chocolate cake castle, then she'd run into her room to write to him. Then she'd work on the shimmering moat of apricot sauce, then slip back to see if he'd answered.

Dear BrooklynBoy, she wrote. **I'm modest about**

some things, but not this: **I make the best fudge brownies on the planet.**

He wrote back almost immediately. **Well,** he said, **it just so happens, I make the best homemade ice cream.**

Jean was loving this. **Ice cream and brownies,** she wrote. **Now that's a good combo.** She took a breath and decided to say what she was thinking. **That's all I'm looking for,** she tapped out. **My own combo. Someone I can bring out the best in, and who brings out the best in me.**

Holly, masquerading as BrooklynBoy, was reading everything her mom wrote. She couldn't help thinking about those words the next day during gym class as she watched Adam across the basketball court. He was watching her, too. This time, when they caught each other looking, they both just smiled.

Holly smiled to herself that night, too, as she lay in bed and stared up at the wall at the princess drawing Adam had given her. It was lit up by a big full moon that shone through her window.

That same moon lit Adam's room, where he lay in bed sketching another Princess Holly picture.

Jean saw the moon, too, as she gazed yearningly out her bedroom window, looking east toward China.

And Ben — the *real* Ben? He was down at the River Bistro, helping Amber go over wedding-cake designs. But something called him to the door of the restaurant. He stood there, staring up at the big full moon, feeling the pull of its force.

15

"Oh, my God!" Holly cried the next day. She was working on the computer while Adam folded laundry in his room. "I'm in the middle of writing my mom an e-mail — and she just logged on!"

Adam came over to see. "IM her," he suggested.

"Should I?" Holly asked.

Adam shrugged. "It'll make Ben seem more real, won't it?"

Holly's heart was beating fast. This would take things to a whole new level. Was she ready? Was Jean ready? Oh, well! She typed something quickly. **Fancy running into you here . . .** Then she closed her eyes for a moment, opened them, and hit SEND.

Two milliseconds later, the reply came back and the conversation began.

Passionate Baker: What time is it there?

Holly panicked. She had no idea what time it was in China.

BrooklynBoy: Late.

Passionate Baker: I thought it would be morning.

"Oops," Holly said out loud.

BrooklynBoy: It is. Late morning. What are you doing?

Passionate Baker: Just thinking.

BrooklynBoy: About what?

Passionate Baker: You'd be bored.

BrooklynBoy: Try me. If I stop replying, you'll know I fell asleep.

Passionate Baker: Well, I have kids. Have I mentioned that?

BrooklynBoy: No. That's great.

Passionate Baker: Two daughters. Seven and sixteen.

BrooklynBoy: They're lucky to have you as a mom.

Passionate Baker: You are the only person on Earth who would say that. And it's just because you haven't met me. I've made so many mistakes.

Holly stared at the screen. Didn't her mom realize that what BrooklynBoy said was true? No matter what, Holly had *always* felt lucky to have Jean as a mom.

BrooklynBoy: Everybody makes mistakes.

Passionate Baker: Yeah, well, I make whoppers. Over and over, and my kids are the ones to suffer. It's not fair.

Holly stared at the screen, feeling a lump begin to grow in her throat. She hated that her mom felt this way. She wanted to reassure her, tell her she'd done a great job raising her and Zoe. But how? What would Ben say?

BrooklynBoy: You haven't been a perfect mother. But it's not a perfect world.

Passionate Baker: Theirs would be closer to perfect if their mom had her act together. This wasn't the plan, you know. I had a big future in mind when I was younger. I was going to be a famous baker, like Julia Child, but with desserts. I was going to go to a fancy cooking school, write cookbooks — make people fall in love with baking again. I had all the applications, too. I was in the middle of filling them out when I learned I was pregnant. I thought it was good news. A baby fit into my happily-ever-after plan just fine. But it didn't fit into the guy's. Or maybe it was me that didn't fit. Whichever. I was on my own.

Wow. Holly sat back in her seat, stunned. She'd never known exactly how much her mom had given up for her and Zoe.

BrooklynBoy: So you had your kid instead of fulfilling your dream.

Passionate Baker: I guess I did.

Holly sat very still for a moment, afraid to ask the question she most wanted to ask. Then she started typing again.

BrooklynBoy: If you had it all to do over, would you have gone to school instead?

Holly waited. Jean didn't answer right away. Then the message came.

Passionate Baker: Life definitely would be easier if I'd done that — gotten my act together first, had kids later. But — those kids wouldn't be Holly and Zoe. And life without Holly and Zoe? I can't even imagine it. That's just no life at all.

Holly stared at the screen, feeling the tears prick at her eyes. She'd always known that her mom loved her — but she'd never known quite how much.

When she arrived home that night, Holly found Jean in the kitchen, watching her electric mixer turn batter around and around. For a few seconds, Holly just stood there watching, as if she'd never really *seen* her mother before.

Then she spotted the contest brochure lying on the kitchen table. She picked it up and looked it over. Then she walked over to her mom, hugged her, and handed her the brochure — and a pen.

Jean smiled. Then, leaving the mixer to do its thing, she began to fill out the form.

Back in her room, Holly sat down for a quick blogging session.

username: GIRL ON THE MOVE

i'm listening to: nothing

current mood: thankful

Special message to all you bloggers out there being raised by single moms: Give the old lady a break. She's doing the best she can.

16

"All right," Jean said, coming into the living room a couple mornings later. It was a Saturday, and Holly and Amy were ready to kick back and relax. At the moment, Holly was French-braiding Amy's hair. "I'm off to Gloria's shower," Jean went on. "Don't burn the place down." She'd already gotten a sitter for Zoe, so Holly could enjoy a day off.

Holly took in her mother's outfit. "Wow," she said, "look at you. Where are they having this shower, the Ritz?"

Jean spun around to show off her dress. "Close to it," she told Holly. "It's at some whoop-de-do restaurant called the River Bistro."

"No!" cried Holly, yanking Amy's braid by mistake.

"Ouch!" yelled Amy.

"I mean," Holly said, trying to cover for herself, "isn't that over everyone's budget?"

Jean nodded. "Yeah, but Gloria's cousin's wife works for their dairy guy so she got a deal on the party room."

Holly looked at Amy.

Amy looked at Holly.

Panic.

Amy stood up. "I've heard their food's really bad," she declared. "Everyone who eats there gets sick. Vomiting for days."

Jean just raised an eyebrow. "I'll take my chances." She kissed Holly good-bye and left. As soon as she closed the door behind her, Holly and Amy swung into action.

"Where is he?" Holly demanded.

"I don't know," Amy said. "Maybe the restaurant, maybe home?"

Holly jumped up and grabbed her jacket and her phone.

"You go to the restaurant," she ordered. "I'll go to his place. Keep your phone *on*."

It wasn't long before Holly found herself in front of a beautiful loft building down by the Brooklyn Bridge. She checked the address she'd felt-tipped onto her palm. Yup. This was it. She pressed the buzzer hard.

"Hello?" Ben's voice came through the speaker.

"Oh, my God, you're there!" Holly was relieved.

"Who is this?" Ben asked.

"It's Holly. Amy's friend."

There was a pause. Then Ben spoke again. "Amy's not here, Holly."

"I know," Holly said. "I'm here to see you."

Another pause, briefer this time. "Come on up," Ben said. "My door's open."

Holly found her way up the stairs and pushed open the door to Ben's apartment. "Hi!" she called as she walked in. She looked around. Wow. What an incredible place! A beautiful kitchen flowed into a living room full of books. Huge bay windows flooded the whole place with light. In the kitchen, spices were lined up in the windows, and garlands of garlic and shiny red hot peppers hung from the ceiling, along with row upon row of gleaming pots and pans. This was a *kitchen*. The kind that really was the heart of a home. It was impressive — but also warm and inviting. Holly ran her hand over the polished stone countertop.

"Whoa," she said under her breath.

"What?" Ben asked. He had put down the crossword puzzle he was working on and now he was standing across the counter from Holly.

"This is the most beautiful kitchen in the whole world," Holly said.

"Yeah," Ben said proudly. "Thank you."

Holly was still gazing around. "I know someone who would kill for this kitchen. I bet Amber likes it a lot, huh?"

"Amber?" Ben asked. "That woman has her stamp over

everything I do, but no, this kitchen is *my* baby." He waited for Holly to state her business, but she seemed mesmerized by her surroundings. "Was there something you wanted to talk to me about?" Ben finally asked.

"Oh!" Holly said. "Yes. Something very important." But she didn't continue.

Ben waited. And waited. "Would you like something to eat or drink?" he offered, trying to be polite.

"How about some Peking duck?" Holly asked, stalling. "I hear that takes, like, a day to prepare."

Ben gave her a quizzical look. "Tell you what," he said. "Have a seat, and I'll get us some sodas, okay?"

The main thing was to *keep* Ben here, away from the restaurant, where Jean would spot her perfect man immediately. "Take your time!" Holly urged. "I read recently that people who rush through their lives get indigestion and memory loss. So — don't rush for me."

Ben looked totally confused. He just waved her into the living room and went to get the sodas.

Holly wandered over to the chair where Ben had been sitting when she came in. When she spotted the crossword lying there, she froze in her tracks. Then she stepped a little closer, just to double-check. Yup. Ben was doing the crossword in pen.

Just then, he came over with two sodas. "Was that slow enough?"

Holly gaped at him. "You do the *Times* crossword. In pen."

"Is that bad?" Ben asked, perplexed.

Holly added it all up. Sensitive nature. Knowledge of women. Gorgeous kitchen. Crosswords in ink. Maybe Ben really *was* Mr. Perfect! How tragic would *that* be, given his relationship with Amber? She squinted at him. "How do you feel about the moon?" she asked.

"I'm sorry?" said Ben, looking more lost than ever.

"Is it just a rock floating in space," Holly clarified her question, "or is it a little bit of magic that comes out every night, even when times are hard, to remind us that every day holds the potential for beauty?"

Ben stared at her. Was this girl a mind reader? "What has Amy told you about me?" he asked, not that he remembered ever sharing his deepest feelings about the moon with his niece.

"Nothing," Holly answered. "She just said you were really smart, and I'm new to town, new school and all, and I don't have a dad to turn to for advice, so I figured I'd ask you for some."

Ben's face cleared. This he could handle. Or at least, he'd try. "Okay," he told her. "I'll help if I can. What is it?"

Holly racked her brain for a problem she could present to Ben. It's something that would take, oh, four or five hours to discuss. "Well, it's no big deal," she began. "It's just — I'm going through my teenage years, and that's confusing.

I'm confused about who I am and what my purpose is in life. I don't know where I want to go to college, or if I should go to college. I'm trying to resist peer pressure to do all sorts of things that I shouldn't do, but some of them I kind of want to do, if you know what I mean?"

Without waiting for Ben's response, she rattled on, "I'm considering piercing my nose, my belly button, and nine other body parts, but my mom said she would kill me so I'm just gonna get a tattoo on my back, well, on my lower back, like, so low I don't think it will actually be on my back but you *will* be able to see it if I wear my pants low enough. I'm just really confused. What do you think I should do?"

She took a deep breath.

Ben just stood there, looking as if he'd been run over by a bus. Before he could say a word, the phone rang. He ran over to grab it, looking happy to get away from Holly and her confusion. "Hello?" he said into the receiver. "Whoa, what? It can't be broken! It's three months old! Okay, calm down. I'll be right there." Hanging up, he reached for his coat. "Problem at the restaurant," he told Holly. "I have to go."

"What!" Holly freaked. "No! You can't!"

"Holly —" Ben tried to sound patient.

"I mean . . ." Holly saw that there was no stopping him. "Can I go with you?"

Ben rolled his eyes. "I guess," he said. "Sure."

One last thing, Holly had to give Amy the heads-up. "Okay," she said. "But can I use your bathroom first?"

"Second door on the left," Ben said, pointing her down the hall. "But be quick. I'll call a cab."

Holly ran into the bathroom, shut the door, and turned on both faucets until they were blasting full force. With that sound to cover her voice, she whipped out her cell phone, dialed, and whispered desperately, "Houston! We have a problem."

Over in front of the bistro, Amy spoke urgently into her phone. "What kind of problem?" she asked.

"The very worst," hissed Holly, with the sound of running water behind her. "He's on his way *now*!"

"Oh, my God!" Amy cried. "What do we do?"

Holly spoke firmly. "We go to Plan B."

"We don't *have* a Plan B!" wailed Amy.

She was right. Holly thought fast. "Create a distraction!" she ordered. "A big one!" Then she pressed END.

Amy looked around wildly, trying desperately to think of something to do. Then she spotted a group of construction workers across the street. Hard-hat-wearing, jackhammer-wrestling, city-dirt-smeared construction workers. Perfect.

Meanwhile, inside the bistro in the party room, which was just off the main room, Gloria was busy opening a huge pile of presents. A table full of women gasped and cheered as she pulled a teeny-tiny nightgown out of a box. "You gotta be kidding me," Gloria said, laughing. "This won't cover anything!"

Dolores smiled. "That's exactly the point," she told her friend.

All the women laughed.

Little did they know that at that very moment, Amy was taping a big sign to the front of the restaurant. FREE BEER AND APPETIZERS FOR JETS FANS! it read. Already, a steady stream of construction workers were making their way across the street. It was like attracting bees to honey.

A few minutes later, Ben and Holly climbed out of the taxi that screeched around a corner and pulled up in front of the restaurant. Ben stared at the sign, scratching his head. Then he reached out and ripped it down.

Too late. At the bar, Lance was already overwhelmed by a loud, happy crowd of guys.

Holly guessed that this was Amy's idea of a distraction. Well, okay, it was working. She raced back to the party room just as Jean was heading for the main room, looking for a waiter so she could order Gloria another mimosa.

"Mom!" Holly said. "Hi!"

Jean looked completely shocked. "Holly! What are you doing here?"

Holly glanced behind her and saw that Amy had positioned herself so that she was hiding Ben from Jean's sight. Excellent. "Well," Holly said, gently but forcefully leading her mom back toward the table in the party room, "I just — missed you so much, Mom." She sat Jean down and slid in next to her.

Jean reached over and felt Holly's forehead. "Are you sick?"

Meanwhile, out at the bar, Lance was trying to deal with a crowd of hungry, thirsty Jets fans. "J-E-T-S! Jets! Jets!" they chanted.

"What is that?" Jean asked, craning her neck to see what all the noise was about.

Holly jumped up to block Jean's view. "Hey, neat," she said, grabbing the wrapped party favor in front of her mom. "Presents!" She opened the box to find a flirty red feather boa.

Out at the bar, Ben gave in. "Okay, just give them one round each," he told Lance. "Fill 'em up and move 'em out. I'll go check that broken oven."

Amy followed Ben as he headed for the kitchen. She saw that he had a clear view straight into the party room — right at Jean's back. Holly and she exchanged panicked looks.

Then it got worse. Jean started to turn around. "Where the heck is that waiter?" she asked.

"Do something!" Holly mouthed to Amy.

Amy swept out an arm and knocked a bowl of nuts off the counter and onto the kitchen floor. They skittered all over the place. "Oops," she said. "Sorry."

Ben looked up from the oven and glared at Amy. He reached for a dustpan and bent to sweep up the nuts — just as Jean stood up, turned around, and headed into the main room.

"Mom!" Holly cried, jumping up to run after her. "I'll find him. You go sit down." Jean wasn't stopping, so Holly ran around and stood right in front of her.

"Holly, what's wrong with you?" Jean was beginning to sound mad.

Across the counter, Amy threw Holly a desperate look. Ben was almost done cleaning up the nuts. He was about to stand up.

"There he is!" Holly shouted, pointing in the other direction. She raced over to a waiter, grabbed him, and dragged both him and her mother back to the party room.

Phew! Crisis averted. But Holly looked around the crowded restaurant — at Ben in the kitchen, the construction workers at the bar, the group of women in the party room — and realized she had to do something else. Something drastic.

Just then, she spotted a book of matches on the bar. Grabbing it, she ran for the bathroom. She shut herself into a stall and lit a match, then held it up high, close to the fire sprinkler.

Chaos! Ringing alarms! Water, water everywhere — streaming from the ceiling! All the customers and employees covered their heads. Amy headed for the party room and directed the guests out the back door, away from the main part of the restaurant.

Success.

But Holly couldn't really enjoy it. She watched as her mother hustled out of the restaurant, red feather boa slung around her neck. Then she looked back at Ben as he moved quickly around in the kitchen, trying to save his equipment from the water. And she felt a huge wave of sadness wash over her.

Back at Amy's, the girls dried themselves off, using every towel in the linen closet.

"That *rocked*!" Amy said. "I swear, the CIA should hire us. Nobody saw anybody! Are we the bomb, or are we the bomb?"

Holly plopped herself down on the couch. "Your uncle does the crossword puzzle in pen," she said.

"*What?*" Amy stared at her.

"And he has a beautiful kitchen."

"So?" Amy had no idea where this was going.

"And he may not have said so out loud," Holly went on, oblivious, "but I *know* he doesn't think the moon is just a rock."

Amy put down her towel. "What are you talking about?"

Holly sighed. "There *is* such a thing as a perfect man. And I know who it is for my mom."

"Who?" asked Amy. She still wasn't getting it.

"Your uncle Ben."

"*What?*" Amy couldn't believe her ears. She hadn't seen this coming, not at all.

"But because of my stupid scheme," Holly said sadly, "they can never meet."

Amy just stood there, shaking her head. "I'm so beyond lost," she admitted.

Holly looked up at her friend. "You were right," she said woodenly. "I never should have bought that orchid. The whole thing was just a colossal mistake."

18

Holly knew there was only one way to fix the mess she'd made. It wouldn't be pleasant, but it had to be done.

Just not by her.

She approached Adam the next day in the art room. He was hanging up wet woodcut prints and didn't see her coming. "I need to ask a huge favor of you," she said, without even saying hello.

He turned to look at her. The girl was a mess. "Frazzled" didn't even begin to describe her. "Hi to you, too," he said.

Holly was too impatient to stop and start all over again. Instead, she got right to the point. "I want you to break up with my mother," she told him.

Adam raised one eyebrow. "When did I start dating her?"

"Not as you," Holly said, exasperated. "As the perfect man. Ben."

Adam turned back to his woodcuts. "No way."

Holly ran around to face him. "Oh, come on, *please?*" she begged. "Just call her tonight at seven, put on a deep voice, and tell her it's over."

Adam did not look convinced. "What's my reason?"

Holly shrugged. "Men never have a reason. They just split."

Adam was a little shocked by how jaded Holly was. "Why can't you just break up by e-mail?" he said. He really wanted nothing to do with this.

"That's too cold," Holly said. "Besides, I just — I want her to hear his voice." She'd thought this all out. Why was Adam resisting?

"It wouldn't be his voice," Adam pointed out. "It would be mine. What with him not *existing* and all."

"You know what I mean," Holly snapped.

Adam thought it over. Holly waited.

"Please, Adam," she finally said, in a softer voice. "If I tell her it was all fake, she'll be crushed. And she'll never forgive me. But if he just dumps her — well — *that* she's used to."

Later that night, Holly stared at the clock in the living room while Jean worked in the kitchen, frosting a cake. Just as the minute hand jumped to seven, the phone rang. Holly dove for it. "Hello?" she said, a little breathlessly. "May I ask who's calling?" Then she covered the phone with her hand. "Mom?" She carried the phone into the kitchen and handed it to Jean.

Jean wiped her hands on a towel and took it. "Hello?" she asked.

Holly slipped back into her bedroom and carefully lifted the receiver so she could listen. There was a huge knot in her stomach. She hated to think how her mom was going to be feeling a few minutes from now. But it was for the best — wasn't it?

"Hi," said Adam-as-Ben. His voice came out a little high, so he lowered it some more. "This is Ben calling." By the word "calling," his voice was as deep as it could get.

"Ben?" Jean sounded shocked. "As in *Ben*, Ben?"

"Um," Adam said, "I think so. How many Bens do you know?"

"None." Jean caught herself. "I mean, one. You. I know you." She paused to take a breath and collect herself. "Wow. Hi. How's China?"

Adam didn't have a clue how China was. "It's very — Chinese," he said finally. "There's a lot of Chinese people here. Chinese food." Argh. He was so lame!

Jean didn't seem to notice. "You're funny," she said, laughing, as she strolled out onto the balcony, phone to her ear. "And you're calling me. From halfway around the world!" She sounded a little choked up.

Adam thought he'd better get right to the point. "Yeah, well," he said, "there was something I wanted to tell —"

But Jean interrupted him. "It's good to finally hear your voice," she said. Her own voice was shaking a little. She sniffed back a tear.

"Wait —" Adam said, sounding a little panicked. "Are you crying?"

In her room, Holly flopped back on her bed. This was *not* going well.

"No, no!" Jean said, even though she was. "I mean — yes. But it's only because I'm happy. I guess you do that to me. You make me happy. You know what I mean?"

Adam, in his room, looked over at his computer. The screensaver was the digital photo he'd taken of Holly. He gazed at her image. "Um, I guess," he said. "Yeah, I do."

In *her* room, Holly sat up and frowned. What was Adam doing? He wasn't supposed to say that.

Jean was talking. "My whole life, everything's been so

messed up. But then I started getting to know you, and I don't know, everything just started feeling . . ." She groped for the word.

Adam was still looking at the picture of Holly. "Clearer?" he suggested.

"Yes!" Jean said. "You know what I mean!"

Holly could not believe what she was hearing. She shook her head.

"Yeah," Adam said. "I do."

Holly mouthed a silent scream. "No, you don't!" Adam had gone totally out of control.

But it got worse. Adam, still gazing at Holly's image, went on. "It's like, all the bad stuff you went through, that you hated along the way — the people who disappointed you, the things that didn't go the way you wanted — suddenly, you feel grateful to them, because they're the things that brought you here. To this."

In her room, Holly was going ballistic. She was going to *kill* Adam.

"*Yes*," Jean breathed. "Exactly."

Adam kept going. "I guess that's just how it is when you — when you —"

"What?" Jean asked.

"Really, really like someone."

That did it. Holly put down the phone and went out into the living room. She slunk down on her hands and knees, behind the sofa so that Jean wouldn't turn around and see her. Suddenly, Zoe jumped on her back. "Give me a ride!" she demanded.

"Not now, Zoe!" Holly whisper-yelled, sitting Zoe back down on the couch with her book. Then she looked down at the floor and saw the phone cord that led out to the balcony. She followed it backward, into Jean's room where it was plugged in.

Out on the balcony, Jean leaned against the door. "So, you like me, huh?" she asked dreamily.

"Yeah, I do," Adam said. He couldn't take his eyes off the picture of Holly. "I might even, I mean, I — uh, I might —"

"You might even *what?*" asked Jean, her voice trembling.

Holly couldn't hear what Adam was saying, but she had a pretty good idea, based on Jean's side of the conversation. It was time for drastic action. With one swift yank, she pulled the phone cord out of the wall.

In his room, Adam spoke into the phone, not knowing it was dead. "I might even . . . love you."

"Hello?" Jean asked. "Hello?"

"What is *wrong* with you?" Holly yelled at Adam, the next day. She'd caught him near his locker, just before the first bell. "That wasn't anywhere *near* what I asked you to do!"

Adam gaped at her. "I got — distracted," he said in a small voice.

"By *what?*" Holly was raging. "A lobotomy? 'Cause short of *that*, short of you telling me someone came in and removed part of your brain, I can't even *begin* to imagine what you were —"

Adam grabbed her by the shoulders.

He leaned in.

He kissed her.

"By you," he said. "I was talking about *you*."

The bell rang and Adam turned and headed down the hall.

And Holly just stood there, her head reeling.

Meanwhile, Jean was dealing with her own love-struck man. The A&P was thronged with shoppers, all of whom were listening to Lenny, who sat in the manager's booth, talking over the PA.

"Attention, shoppers," he said. "Need a little pick-me-up? Then stop on over to our Coffee Corner and try a half-caf caramel machiatto." He was staring straight at Jean, down in the bakery. "But remember," he warned. "Coffee can be hot. It can have an intensity like you've never felt before, searing deep into your flesh . . ."

By now, he had the complete attention of everyone in the store.

". . . your tender, vulnerable, easily hurt flesh," he went on, still staring at Jean. The listening shoppers followed his gaze and saw Jean standing in the bakery. She could feel their stares, and she wished she could disappear, just melt into a puddle of vanilla frosting.

"So be sure you ask for a protective sleeve for your coffee cup," Lenny finished. "And maybe pick up another one . . . to slip over your heart."

Ouch. Jean felt his pain. In fact, she'd felt that kind of pain over and over and over, every single time she'd been dumped.

"What's with lover-boy?" Dolores asked.

Jean's shoulders were slumped. "I told him I met someone else."

Gloria's eyes lit up. "You did? Who?"

Jean didn't answer.

"Oh, no," Dolores said. "Not Mr. Where-the-heck-are-you-dot-com."

Jean bristled. "He's in China," she informed her friend. "And we have a connection."

Dolores shook her head. "Yeah, via satellite. That ain't a relationship, girl."

"It could be," Jean said, thinking of the phone call the night before. "I mean, it will be."

"When?" Dolores demanded.

Jean just bit her lip.

Dolores wasn't having any of it. "Jean," she said. "Lenny isn't perfect, but he's here, and he's real. For all you know, Mr. No-Show is a fat old lady in Dubuque."

Jean thought about that. She thought long and hard, all the way through her shift, and all the way home.

"Mom?" Holly asked that evening. Jean was settled in on the sofa, doing the crossword. Zoe lay on the floor, reading. All was peaceful. Holly figured this was probably as good a time as any to confess that she'd made the whole Ben thing up. That was all she could do now, since the big breakup hadn't worked.

"Yeah?" Jean asked, still looking down at her puzzle.

Holly took a breath. "Remember, um . . . when we first got here and you were feeling so lousy?"

Now Jean was looking at her. "What about it?" she asked. She could see that her daughter was struggling with something important.

"Well, the thing is," Holly began, "I . . . um . . . I hated seeing you like that —"

Just then, she was interrupted by the sound of a loud power chord. The screeching notes of an electric guitar, coming from the street below.

Zoe sat up. "What was *that?*"

Holly, Zoe, and Jean went out to the balcony and looked down.

There on the sidewalk was Lenny, wearing his very best Styx jean jacket.

He was playing an electric guitar plugged into a portable amp, and he was singing. Badly.

It was a Styx song. What else? The one he'd sung to Jean at the tribute concert.

He began wailing so off-key that it was actually kind of sweet, and staring soulfully up at Jean. "'Baby, please, believe that it's true, babe, I love you.'" Lenny sang the last line meaningfully. "'Babe, I want to MARRY YOU!'"

Zoe broke out into giggles.

Holly broke out into a cold, horrified sweat.

Jean looked . . . touched.

Lenny bent over the guitar, wailing into a long, passionate guitar solo. When he finished, he took off the guitar, gazed up at Jean, and began to climb up the fire escape.

Yikes. Lenny was not cut out for climbing fire escapes.

"Oh, my," Jean said as she watched him struggle up the ladders.

"He's gonna break something," Holly said.

"S-P-A-S-T-I-C," spelled Zoe.

Finally, Lenny reached the top of the fire escape. From there, he had to climb over a railing and make his way across a bay window in order to reach Jean on the balcony.

By the time he got there, he was sweating unattractively, not to mention wheezing. He pulled a small, black velvet box out of his pocket. "Marry . . . me!" he gasped.

Jean looked at Holly and Zoe. "Girls," she said. "Privacy."

This was no time to argue. Besides, Holly did not really want to witness this car wreck. Holly grabbed Zoe and pulled her into their bedroom.

Ten minutes later, Jean opened the door.

Holly studied her mother's face, looking for clues. "You said no, right?" she asked. "Please, oh, God, please, tell me you said no."

"I said I'd think about it," Jean answered.

Holly groaned. A vivid picture of Lenny as her and Zoe's new dad filled her mind. "*What* is there to think about?"

Jean held out the box, showing them the engagement ring. Zoe squinted at it. "Is there a jewel in there?"

Holly didn't even try to play find-the-diamond. "Mom!" she said. "You can't say yes!"

"Actually," Jean corrected her daughter, "I can."

"But Lenny's not your soul mate!" she wailed. "Ben is!"

Jean looked thoughtful. "Ben is in China. Maybe. Who really knows?" Her eyes grew distant. "The only thing I know for sure about Ben is that he's a beautiful idea. But you can't grow old with a beautiful idea."

"But," Holly spluttered, "he gave you orchids, and great music!" What was she doing? A half hour earlier, she'd been ready to tell her mom that Ben didn't exist.

Jean just looked back at her calmly. "And Lenny gave me a ring," she said.

Holly shook her head. She could not believe her mother. "Why do you have to be so desperate?" she demanded.

Jean winced. Then she rallied. "It's easy for you to judge, Holly," she said. "You haven't had to make your way through life, with kids, all alone, with nobody to turn to for help." Her voice grew firmer. "Now, I'm not complaining — I made my bed — but I have been slugging it out all by myself for a heck of a long time. And you girls are the best thing that ever happened to me, but in the blink of an eye you'll be gone, and I will be one hundred percent alone."

Holly was trying to really *hear* what her mother was saying. So far, she understood. But then Jean went on. "Lenny is a sweet man," she said. "Maybe he'll be different than the others. I don't want to wind up sad and lonely."

"But not *Lenny*, Mom!" Holly said, unable to stop herself. "Someone better will turn up, if you just wait —"

"How long?" Jean interrupted. "'Cause, call me crazy, but I think seventeen years is long enough." With that, she turned and left the room.

Holly watched her go. Again she pictured Lenny, this time at the altar, waiting for Jean, his bride. No! Something had to be done. Something drastic. She thought as hard as she ever had. Then she strode over to the door and locked it from the inside. "Keep that locked until I come back," she instructed Zoe.

Grabbing her cell phone, she climbed out onto the fire escape. This time, she headed up one flight, so she'd be out of earshot. She sat down on the landing, took out her cell phone, and stared at it for a full minute. Then she dialed.

Downstairs, Jean walked into her bedroom and picked up the phone. "Hello?"

Holly hadn't quite figured out her accent. What was supposed to sound Chinese came out sounding more like

Chinese-French-Australian-Portuguese-Norwegian. "I am calling for Miss Jean Hamilton," she said.

There was a brief pause. "Yes, this is Jean," came the cautious answer.

"I am the secretary for Mr. Ben," Holly began.

"*Really?*" Jean asked. She seemed to be reacting to the weird accent. "Are you sick?"

"No," Holly shot back. "I'm from China."

Her mom took that in. "Are you maybe from China *and* sick?"

Holly decided it was best to give in. "Yes, very sick," she said, letting out a fake cough. "Have Chinese flu you hear about. Very bad." She coughed again.

"The bird one?" Jean asked.

Holly needed this conversation to move on. "No, no, worse," she said, coughing some more and hoping nobody in the upstairs apartment was listening. "But this does not matter. What matters is" — she threw in a cough or two — "he come back and want to see you."

"Really?" Jean sounded a little too skeptical.

Holly decided to push it. "I need answer now," she said, forgetting the cough for a moment. "I must go see a doctor. Yes or no? You want to see him?"

"Oh," said Jean. "Yes. Sure. Yes, I do."

Victory! "How does tomorrow afternoon under the Brooklyn Bridge sound?" Holly added a cough or two to punctuate her question.

"Romantic," Jean answered.

"Excellent," Holly said, getting ready to hang up. "Four o'clock." She coughed three times, for luck. "He'll see you there."

Holly hung up and snuck down the fire escape, far enough to see her mother through the bedroom window. Jean sat there for a second looking stunned. Then she flopped down on the bed, still holding the phone and staring at the ceiling in wonder.

Holly looked at her mom, then down at the cell phone in her hand. What could she possibly have been thinking? There was absolutely no way out of this one.

Twelve hours later, the next morning, Holly still wasn't sure exactly what she was going to do. Or, at least, she knew what she was going to do. She just didn't know if it would work. But she had to try. She sat at her desk, watching as the printer spit out every e-mail Jean had ever written to "Ben." While she watched, the IM bleep sounded. She turned to her computer and saw a message from Adam. **Holly,** it said. **Where are you? Been trying to reach you.**

Adam. Holly had barely had a second to think about him.

And yet — she'd been thinking of him every second.

Another IM came on. **Filing a missing persons report!**

Holly stared at the computer screen, tempted to respond. But there was no time for that. Not now. She closed her laptop and gathered up all the e-mails, stuffing them into an envelope.

Fifteen minutes later, she ran into the River Bistro, the envelope in her hand. "Where's Ben?" she asked Lance, who was wiping down the bar. "I have to talk to him. It's an emergency!"

"Too late, kiddo," Lance said calmly. "He's already gone."

"Where?" Holly demanded, her heart sinking.

Lance rolled his eyes. "The almighty wedding."

"Wedding!" This was worse than Holly could have imagined. "What wedding?"

"Well," Lance said, as if it were obvious, "Amber and —"

"Amber?" Holly asked. "*Amber?*"

"I know," Lance said sympathetically. "He didn't really want to do it, but she's hard to say no to."

"But — but —" Holly didn't understand. Wouldn't Lance have been invited? "Why aren't you there?"

"*Exactly*," Lance said.

"Where is it?" Holly could see that Lance was hurt, but she had no time to cheer him up. "Where's the wedding?"

"Liberty Grand Hotel," Lance said.

Before he even finished the words, Holly was out the door, envelope in hand.

Holly ran into the hotel at full tilt. She didn't have to ask anyone where the wedding was — it was obvious. It had taken over the place. It was like The Wedding That Ate Brooklyn. Guests in formal attire overflowed the room, and huge, splashing fountains flanked the altar. Flowers? There were flowers enough for a hundred weddings. Up front, the bride and groom stood in a perfect little gazebo, facing the priest. Holly could see Amber's face. She couldn't see Ben's.

"If anyone present knows a reason why these two cannot be lawfully wedded," the priest was saying as Holly ran in, "speak now or forever hold your peace."

A shrill blast pierced the air.

It was Holly, blowing on the whistle attached to her key chain. "He can't marry her!" she shouted.

Every single guest turned to look at the insane girl in the middle of the aisle. Their faces were a study in shock.

"He has to marry my mother!" Holly went on, her shout slightly toned down.

At that, the guests gasped.

So did Ben. Holly saw him up front, dressed in a tux. He was surrounded by three other guys, who were all in tuxes, as well. The groomsmen. Ben was staring back at her as she continued. "Maybe he doesn't know it yet, but he will when he reads these!" She brandished the envelope, then realized she should explain what it contained.

"Pages and pages of proof," she said, "that she's his soul

mate. And right now, she's waiting under the Brooklyn Bridge to meet you — and when you do, you'll see how perfect you are for each other." Maybe she wasn't making any sense. Was that why everyone kept staring? But Holly had to go on. "How you both do crosswords in pen, and know what a kitchen should feel like, and what the moon really is . . ." All this time, Holly was walking up the aisle, coming closer and closer to Ben. "And how without even meeting her, you picked her favorite song, and made her happier than she's ever — "

Suddenly, she realized there was something wrong.

Among the men Ben was standing with was one with a white boutonniere instead of a red one. And his tux was a little different, too. Fancier. And he was standing right next to Amber.

Why?

Because, Holly slowly realized, he was the groom. Not Ben.

Amber wasn't marrying Ben. She was marrying this man with a goatee, this man Holly had never seen before in her whole entire life. Ben was just a groomsman. Or maybe best man. But. He. Was. Not. The. Groom.

Holly couldn't stop her train of thought quite in time. "Happier than . . . she's . . . ever . . . been," she petered out, just as a furious-looking Amber hauled off and slapped her fiancé across the face.

"Ow!" The poor man turned and glared at Holly.

"Um," Holly said, realizing that an explanation of some sort might be in order. "I was — I was looking for the Silverman wedding. My bad. Carry on."

With that, she slunk back up the aisle, avoiding the eyes that burned into her from every side.

22

"Hey!"

Holly knew that voice. She turned to face Ben, who had followed her into the hotel lobby. Her face was burning. She could not remember ever having been quite so embarrassed. "Sorry," she whispered. "I made a mistake."

Ben's face was red, too. He was furious. "Understatement of the year," he said. "What the heck were you thinking?"

It was time for the truth. "That you were the one marrying Amber."

"Me?" Ben's jaw dropped open.

"Lance said —" Holly began, but Ben interrupted her.

"Amber's my friend! I'm catering her wedding. Or what's

left of it." Ben shook his head in amazement. "What was that all about?" he asked.

Holly thought he would never ask. She shoved the envelope full of e-mails into his hand. "Read these," she said.

"That's not an answer." But Ben took the envelope.

"Yes, it is," Holly told him. "Read them, and you'll see. There's someone you have to meet."

"Hi, Mom."

Jean looked *beautiful*. At least she did while the light of hope was still in her eyes. When she saw Holly approach the stone bench where she sat waiting, under the Brooklyn Bridge, her expression went through a million changes.

And ended at *sad*.

Jean's face showed, suddenly, that she knew this afternoon was not going to end the way she had wished it would. Holly felt like a dog with its tail between its legs as she walked up to her mom.

"Holly?" Jean asked. "What are you doing here?"

Holly's voice was choked. "I didn't want you to think you'd been stood up. He's not coming."

Jean stared at her blankly. "How do you know? Wait — how did you even know I was —"

Holly flinched. This just hurt way too much. "I know because . . . because —"

"Because what?" Jean demanded.

"I . . . I made him up," Holly blurted.

Jean's mouth opened, but no words came out.

Holly knew she had to say more. "The, um, the flowers, the letters — the e-mails. Everything." She looked into her mother's eyes and saw the tears forming.

Jean couldn't seem to catch her breath. "The phone call?"

Holly nodded. "That was a friend of mine."

Jean looked totally and completely stunned.

"It wasn't all made up," Holly rushed ahead. "I mean, there was a man. There *is* — and most of the things I wrote came from him —"

Now Jean looked as if she might be about to hurl. "There's a man out there, laughing at me, too?"

"No!" Holly felt like crying. "He doesn't know. He thought —"

But her mother wasn't even listening. "My God, Holly. How could you be so cruel?"

"I wasn't trying to be cruel," Holly answered in a tiny voice. "I wanted to . . . I don't know —"

"Have a good laugh at my expense?" Jean asked, her eyes flashing.

"No!" This was the hardest thing Holly had ever done. "I did it to make you happy." Why couldn't her mother understand?

Jean laughed, a weird, barking kind of laugh. "Boy," she said. "You've got a lot to learn about happiness."

"Yeah," said Holly under her breath. "I wonder why that is."

Jean heard her loud and clear. "What is that supposed to mean?" She glared at Holly.

Holly glared right back. "You haven't exactly given me a road map, Mom," she said.

Jean sat back on the bench. "Oh, so this is *my* fault? I've brought this humiliation upon myself because, what, we've moved around a little?"

"A *little?*"

"Whatever," Jean said, flinging her hands in the air. "A lot. You never said you minded."

"Yes, I did," Holly told her. As long as they were getting it all out, she might as well say it. "You just never heard anything if it wasn't about you."

For a second, Jean was quiet. Then she reacted. "That is not true! I hear everything you say to me."

"You hear," Holly said quietly. "But you don't listen. You never listen to what I want."

Jean gave her a curious look. "Fine. Tell me. What do you want?"

Holly drew in a breath. This was something she'd been

thinking about. A lot. "I want a mom who sees in herself what Zoe and I see every day," she began. "That she's talented and funny and pretty and cooks great and dances great and everything about her is great." She began to talk faster, gathering steam. "That's what you've been like, Mom, ever since you got those flowers. And, okay, maybe the perfect man wasn't real. But the perfect *you* was."

Jean looked at Holly for a moment, and the hurt in her eyes was so huge that Holly wanted to cry.

Then Jean stood up and walked away.

Just like that.

Holly watched her mother go, feeling as if her whole world was crashing.

24

Dinner that night was a very, very quiet affair. Jean didn't speak. Neither did Holly.

"S-I-L-E-N-C-E," Zoe spelled.

Holly didn't even look up from her plate. How had things gotten so bad? Could they get any worse?

They could. The next afternoon, as Holly was heading home from school, she came across Adam. He was clearly waiting for her.

"Hi," she said.

"Hi," he answered.

Ugh. Everything was stiff and weird. "Um," Holly said

after a moment, "I'm sorry I didn't call you back. I've been really busy —"

Adam wasn't even listening to her lame excuses. "I drew you something," he interrupted. He handed her a picture.

Holly looked down at it. Another Princess Holly drawing. But this one was really disturbing. Princess Holly had fifteen arms, like an overgrown octopus. They were all pushing away from her, as if she were being attacked by an invisible enemy.

"Another side of Princess Holly," Adam explained, in answer to her quizzical look. "I decided she doesn't need an army to protect her. No one can get close enough to hurt her in the first place."

Holly had been holding back tears for a long time. Now they started to well up in her eyes. She took one last look at the drawing and shoved it back into Adam's hands. Then she took off running.

"Holly, wait!" Adam called. But it was too late. She'd already disappeared around the corner.

"Ask me what I want," Holly demanded, bursting into the apartment.

Jean was folding laundry in the living room, making neat piles along the back of the couch. "What?" she asked.

Holly was impatient. "Don't think about you, think about me. Ask me what I want."

Jean still didn't understand where this was going. But she decided to play along. "What do you want?"

Holly stood in the middle of the room, arms folded. "I want to move," she said. "I hate this place. I'm over it. I want our next adventure. And I want it now." She was fighting back tears. "We've moved for *you* more times than I can count. I want, just once, for us to move for me." She didn't want to beg, but she couldn't hide the pleading in her voice. "Please?"

A few days later, Adam rang the bell at Holly's apartment. Jean answered the door. "Is Holly home?" Adam asked.

"She's out getting packing boxes," Jean said, shoving back the kerchief that covered her hair. She was in the midst of packing up the kitchen things. She didn't know who this boy was, but just then, she didn't have time to get acquainted.

"What? Why?" Adam asked, not getting it.

"We're moving," Jean explained. "To Arizona. Red Rocks."

Adam's face fell.

Jean felt bad for him. "You want her to call?" she asked gently.

"No," Adam said, knowing she wouldn't. "Um, that's okay. Can you give this to her?" He handed Jean a large envelope. "And tell her she only saw one side of the drawing."

Jean took the envelope and turned it over in her hands. "Okay," she said. "Thanks."

When she headed back upstairs, Jean put the envelope on Holly's bed. Then she got back to work.

After only a short break for another silent dinner, Jean worked steadily for a few more hours. By around midnight, she was nearly done. The only thing left to pack was her vase.

She dumped the flowers out of it, wrapped it up in the tired old reused bubble wrap, and looked around for the packing tape. The tape was nowhere to be seen.

Jean tiptoed into the girls' room. Holly was sacked out,

tired from helping Zoe pack her stuff. Jean spotted the packing tape on top of a box. As she picked it up, she noticed Holly's trash can next to the box. On top of the garbage was the envelope that boy Adam had brought over.

Jean took the envelope into the living room and opened it. Her eyes grew wide when she saw Princess Holly with all the arms. Then she turned the picture over. On the other side, the princess figure was using her arms in a different way. Instead of pushing invisible enemies away, she was embracing someone, with every one of her fifteen arms. It was a prince.

A prince who was staring into the princess's eyes.

A prince who looked an awful lot like Adam.

Over at his house, Adam was lying in bed. He wasn't sacked out like Holly, though. He was thinking. Mulling things over.

Bumming.

Suddenly, he heard his computer bleep. An IM! He jumped out of bed and crossed to his desk in one giant step, his heart pounding.

The message was from Holly.

Hollygirl: Nice drawing. Thank you.

Adam's heart pounded even harder. He rushed to respond, getting all the letters wrong at first.

Adamink: I was inspired.

He thought for a second.

Adamink: I miss you. Why'd you bug out on me?

Hollygirl: I think you make me scared.

Adam could hardly believe his eyes. She was finally admitting it! Little did he know that Holly still lay sleeping in her bed. Her messages were being sent by Jean, who sat at the computer in the darkened apartment, the picture of Princess Holly and Prince Adam at her elbow, her sleeping daughters behind her.

Adamink: News flash. Everyone's scared. That's no reason to run away.

Hollygirl: It's what my mom does.

Adamink: And you want to end up like your mom? Some role model.

There was no answer. Adam couldn't have known that Jean, staring at the screen, was taking that hard. She looked around at the packed-up boxes. Looked at Holly, sleeping with a frown on her face.

Adam took a deep breath and decided to go for it. What did he have to lose? He might as well tell her how he felt.

Adamink: I heard once that love is friendship on fire. That's how I feel about you. . . . Do you really have to go?

26

Jean went straight up to Lenny when she arrived at work the next day. Digging into her purse, she pulled out the ring he'd given her and handed it to him, without a word. He stared at it without taking it.

"You want a bigger ring?" he asked.

Jean shook her head. "It's not the ring. You're a good man, Lenny, a decent man, and you will make some woman out there very happy."

Lenny was looking at her in disbelief. "I don't want what's out there," he told her. "I want what's in here. You."

"No, you don't," Jean said.

"Yeah, I do." Lenny sounded positive.

"You don't."

"I do."

"Please, Lenny —" Jean began.

"I know what I want," he insisted, "and I want —"

"Lenny!" Jean had to stop him. "Lenny, you don't rock my world. I'm sorry." She shoved the ring into his hand and left him standing there, looking as if he'd been punched in the stomach.

Later that day, back at the apartment, Holly let herself in. She'd just come back from a long walk around the neighborhood, perhaps her last one. Zoe ran up to her. "Guess what?" she asked joyfully. "I get to be in the spelling bee!"

That's when Holly noticed that Jean was busy in the living room, unpacking all the boxes they'd just filled up. "What are you doing?" she asked her mom.

"Unpacking," Jean said, as if it were obvious.

"Yeah," Holly said. "But why? We all agreed. It's time for a new adventure."

Jean shook her head. "This is our new adventure, Holly," she said softly. "Staying is our new adventure."

Holly was stunned. Unbelieving. How could this be? "Why can't you ever do what I want!" she shouted. Then she ran to her room and slammed the door behind her. She dove onto the bed and buried her head in her pillow.

A few moments later, Jean came in.

"I want to be alone," Holly said, through her pillow.

Jean sat down on the bed, pulled the pillow away, and smoothed Holly's hair. "Don't be ridiculous," she said. "Nobody wants to be alone."

"I do!" Holly yelled. "I don't want to see anybody!" She was crying. "I told you — I'm done with these people. I want *new* ones!"

Jean thought that over. "Unfortunately, honey-pie," she said finally, "new people only stay new for a day. After that, they're just people who will excite you, and disappoint you, and scare you a little bit. . . ." She looked thoughtful. "And boy, I know how tempting it is to run away when that happens. But after fifteen years of doing that, I'm starting to realize it doesn't get you much."

Holly was listening, but she didn't respond.

Jean went on. "Oh, it's a good way of avoiding things," she said, "but the problem is, you end up avoiding yourself as well. And the people you love. You end up avoiding life."

Jean played with a tendril of Holly's hair. It was almost as if she were talking to herself. "So I've decided to start setting a new example for you girls. I'm gonna try showing you what sticking around looks like. We're gonna dig in here. Really get to know people. Let people get to know us."

Jean got up and went over to Holly's desk, where Adam's drawing still lay. "I don't promise to be any good at it, but I'm gonna try," she said. "Because I want you and Zoe to be better at this than I am. I want you to learn how to let people in." She looked down at the picture. "He's a sweet boy," she finished. "I think it would be worth it."

Holly rolled over in bed and looked at Jean. What was her mom talking about?

Jean handed her the picture. "Turn it over," she said. "Everything always has two sides."

"Anyone know where I can find a really good jouster?" Holly asked, coming up to the booth where Adam sat. She was at the Westside Convention Center, which was currently hosting the Comic Book Convention. The place was hopping! The aisles were full of comic book geeks, collectors, kids, and curious visitors. Holly had used the convention guide to find her way through the maze of booths to the one where Adam sat, drawing.

Adam looked up, startled. When he saw her, a slow smile spread across his face. "Hi," he said.

"Hi," Holly answered, smiling back.

"You came."

"Yeah," Holly said. "Minus a few hands." She was thinking of the fifteen-armed princess.

Adam grinned. "Think of all the money you'll save on gloves."

They stood and smiled at each other for a moment.

Then Adam stood up and came around to her side of the booth, and leaning toward her, he kissed her.

And for the first time, Holly kissed him back.

28

Over the next few weeks, a lot happened besides kissing. Jean entered — and *won* — the baking contest, which meant she now had a brand-new job as a pastry chef. Zoe entered — and *won* — the spelling bee. And Ben happened to come across an envelope that he'd left in his tux jacket way back on the day of Amber's wedding. An envelope full of very, very interesting e-mails.

One day not long after that, Holly took Ben on a walk. They stopped in front of a little restaurant/bakery on a side street and looked through the window. There, just inside, was a curly-haired blond woman hard at work. She looked beautiful and competent in her white uniform as she arranged little swan-shaped puff pastries on a plate. "That's her," Holly said. For the first time, Ben was able to put a face to the name on the e-mails he'd been reading and rereading. He took a good look, and when he turned around to thank her, Holly was already gone.

Ben pushed the door open, making the bell tinkle. A salesgirl smiled from behind the counter. "May I help you?" she asked.

"Word has it I can find the best fudge brownies in the world here," Ben said.

Jean, over by another counter, suddenly stood up straight. She recognized those words. She turned to look at Ben. Oh, my. It really was him! "I'll take this," she said to the salesgirl. Jean reached up to a shelf and put a brownie into a waxed paper bag. Stepping over to Ben, she handed it to him with a brilliant smile. "On the house," she said.

"Oh, no," Ben said. "I have to pay you somehow." He smiled his most charming smile. "Dinner, maybe?"

Jean's eyes widened. "I don't even know you."

"I'm not so sure about that," Ben said.

Jean wasn't quite ready to believe this was really happening. "Is this a joke?" she asked.

"No," Ben said. Then he quoted her again. "I'm just looking for someone I can bring out the best in, and who brings out the best in me."

Jean smiled.

"I thought I might find it here," Ben finished.

Jean was melting. But she stopped herself. "That's very sweet," she said. "But — I don't think so."

Ben looked surprised. "Are you dating someone?"

"Actually, no," Jean said. "For once in my life, I'm not. And I think I should keep it this way, at least until I get my feet back on the ground." She stopped. "Or — until I get them on the ground for the first time ever."

"I see," Ben said. But he didn't turn to go.

"Nothing personal," Jean offered.

"Of course," Ben agreed.

They stood there, taking each other in. It was obvious that they couldn't stop looking at each other.

"You know," Ben said finally. "I should probably take a dating moratorium, too."

Jean nodded. "I recommend it," she said.

"Clean-out-the-closet sort of thing," Ben went on.

"Good idea."

They were still staring at each other.

"Get my head straight," Ben finished.

"Exactly," Jean agreed.

With that, Ben nodded, took his brownie, and began to walk toward the door. "So, pick you up Saturday at eight?" he asked as he reached for the handle.

"Perfect," said Jean.

29

That night, Holly sat at her desk looking at the proofs of her class picture. She laughed as she remembered the moment it had been snapped. The photographer had just told her to say "cheese" when Adam and Amy jumped into the frame. All three of them were smiling like mad, but Holly's smile was the widest and happiest by far.

Holly smiled now as she tapped out the final entry to her blog.

username: GIRL ON THE MOVE

i'm listening to: a mix my boyfriend made

current mood: content

Just wanted everyone out there to know that GIRL ON THE MOVE has stopped moving. I painted my room. I even hung some pictures. Can you imagine that? How permanent. I used a nail and everything. So, from now on, you can find me in cyberspace at my new permanent address: PRINCESSHOLLY@brooklyn.net.

PS: Yeah, that's my name. Holly.